I0666940

Beyond the Black Sea

Book Two: Activation Series

M Joseph Murphy

Beyond the Black Sea

Cover design by M Joseph Murphy
M Joseph Murphy's Official Website: mjosephmurphy.info

First Edition: June 2014

Works by M Joseph Murphy

ACTIVATION SERIES
Council of Peacocks
Beyond the Black Sea
Terra Incognita (Coming 2015)

SWORD OF KASSANDRA SERIES
A Fallen Hero Rises
Demons of DunDegore (Coming Sept 2014)

Dedication

This book is Whitley Strieber, a true pioneer. Your fiction inspired me to write. Your non-fiction kept me sane. You're a true hero.

"If you want to know the outcome of a game before the game has even started, you need to control each side."
- *David Icke, Children of the Matrix*

"That which is imagined can never be lost."
- *Clive Barker, Weaveworld.*

Chapter One

Wisdom teleported into the United Nations for his 3:00 p.m. meeting. Events around the world had escalated, necessitating the formation of a special committee on the Orphean invasion. He was 20 minutes early but there was a conversation he needed to have before the meeting started. He stepped out of his teleportation field – a circle of bright yellow light – into an executive washroom on the third floor of the Conference Building. With a wave of his hand, he closed the portal. He turned and stared intently at the large mirror above the row of sinks.

"I know you can see me." Wisdom straightened his tie. "I have a message for you. I'm done waiting for you to make your next move. The next move is mine. And you won't see it coming until it's too late."

He waited for a response. When no message reply came from the other side of the mirror, he wasn't surprised. The Orpheans were not fond of direct confrontation.

He left the bathroom and headed towards the meeting room. Security was on high alert. Wisdom saw more armed guards than at previous meetings. It was a good sign. Maybe world leaders were starting to appreciate the risk level.

He stood outside the chamber waiting for the meeting to start. A familiar face approached him, a tall brown-haired man in a dark suit. Gabriel Wainright was the Canadian representative from Candleworks, an international agency devoted to stopping Orphean threats.

Gabriel extended his hand. Wisdom shook it firmly.

"Are we the first here?" Gabriel looked past Wisdom at the closed door to the meeting room.

"Hardly." Wisdom pointed at the door and sighed, annoyed. "The members from the Security Council are in there having their own meeting before we enter."

Gabriel nodded. "Typical. So much for an equal seat at the table. You'd think after what happened at the Vatican they'd be more open."

"This IS them being more open. At least they've stopped ignoring the problem."

"True." Gabriel looked over his shoulder and waved at three women, also dressed in dark suits, who walked towards them. "Here come the other representatives. How did you manage to get through security so quickly?"

Wisdom rolled his eyes. "I don't do security checks. They're stupid. I could blow up this whole building if I wanted to with a blink of my eyes. I don't need weapons."

Several security guards nearby stood up taller, hands a little closer to their weapons.

Gabriel laughed nervously and waved at the guards. "Ixnay on the hreattnay. Or is that reathrnay?"

"You're horrible at Pig Latin. Why do you always try to work it into a conversation?"

Gabriel shrugged. "If you can't have fun with words, what's the point in living?"

The meeting room door opened. Wisdom allowed the Candleworks representatives to enter before him. The seating was assigned. There was no reason to rush.

After several minutes of obligatory small talk, everyone sat and the guards closed the doors again.

At the head of the table sat Penny Dulany, the woman chosen as chair of the special committee. Wisdom had known her since she was a child. Though in her late fifties, Penny looked ten years younger. Her amazing smile could fill up any room. Today, her face was drawn and her eyes uncharacteristically dull.

"We've had news from China." Penny motioned to one of the assistants at the back of the room. He proceeded to distribute manila folders to everyone around the table. "These are pictures from Beijing. The Council of Peacocks attacked a safe house where we'd found and harbored ten Anomalies. All were taken. As you can see in the photos, we paid a high cost."

Wisdom opened his folder and flipped through several black and white photos. Each showed a body.

"How many did we lose?" This came from one of Gabriel's counterparts at Candleworks. Her name was Dr. Melinda Uyldert from the U.K. With her short blond hair, she looked like a young Helen Mirren.

"Forty soldiers." Penny took a deep breath. "Amazing how calling them soldiers is supposed to make it easier to lose them. Soldiers. Like they're not people." She pushed her shoulders back and sat up a little straighter. "Unfortunately, we have more bad news. We don't have all the details but it appears a band of Edimmu attacked a Sasquatch settlement in Tibet."

Wisdom groaned. "Don't call them that. It's a silly name."

Penny threw her hands in the air. "Fine. Lemurians. Whatever you want to call them. Here's the problem. Several shell-shocked survivors wandered into a tourist area. As you can imagine, their appearance started a riot. Thanks to smart phones, that led to dozens of videos uploaded to the Internet before we could rein them in."

Mischa Fradkov, from Russia, cleared his throat. "As you Americans say, the genie is out of the bottle. We cannot put it back. We will go on TV in a few hours to acknowledge the Lemurians are real."

"You can't do that." Wisdom leaned forward. "They'll be hunted. Candleworks promised to ensure their safety in exchange for the barrier technology that blocks Orphean communications. You're in debt to them for half the projects at the Black Pyramid."

"We know, Wisdom." Shaun Brennan, head of the CIA, hung his head. "The president is meeting with advisors right now on how to handle this. It can't be stopped. Too much evidence to bury, even for us."

Wisdom frowned. "Can't we just kill all the witnesses?"

Penny snorted and waved her hand dismissively. "There are thousands of witnesses."

"Since when has that stopped China?" Wisdom asked.

"I resent the accusation." This came from the Chinese representative, Geng Huichang. "My people do not condone murder."

Wisdom glanced around the room. "Who are you trying to fool? There are no cameras here and everyone in this room knows the Chinese are never afraid to make the hard calls."

Fradkov motioned for Huichang to remain calm, then turned to Wisdom. "This time the hard call is choosing truth. At least a version of it. We have too many battles, Wisdom. We can't fight another."

"Besides," Brennan said, "if the Council keeps on the way it has been, Sasquatch will be the least of our worries."

Penny turned to Wisdom. "Has there been any sign of the alien with the gold ring? Defta…what's his name?"

Wisdom smirked. "It's Defksquar. Rhymes with Deathstar."

"You're such a geek." Penny took a deep breath. "You know what I'd like? An enemy named Bob. Why do villains always have such weird names?"

Huichang raised his hand to interject. "Perhaps on his planet, we are the ones with strange names."

Penny nodded. "Good point."

"There's been no sign of him," Wisdom said. "I've been monitoring the two dimensional gates we found, the one in Windsor, Canada, and the other in Thessaloniki, Greece. Nothing. But there may be other gates. We know the Orpheans can travel through mirrors into our world. For all we know, they're moving Defksquar between our world and his. Defksquar also hasn't approached my student, Josh, but we have to assume he's still important to their plans."

Penny motioned once more for her aide. "There's one last thing. Mr. Icke has resurfaced. He claims to have proof of the reptilian agenda. Sources tell us he has a body."

"Damn it!" Wisdom pounded the table. "I thought I had him killed."

Penny smiled. "My father was right about you. Is that your solution to everything? You know, Wisdom, some things cannot be solved with murder."

Wisdom wrinkled his nose. "Nonsense."

Penny threw up her hands again. "You're impossible. Perhaps it's time we leave Mr. Icke alone. He was right, after all, about the reptilians. At least partially."

Wisdom leaned forward. "Exactly. Why do you think I want him dead? You think people will panic over Lemurians? Just imagine if they have proof of shapeshifting reptilians. On another note, I may have some good news."

"Formidable." This was the representative from France, Jean-Yves Ledrec. "We could use some. Have you found this man you search for, Richard Wilkinson?"

Wisdom rubbed his forehead. "Not yet. But we have found several other senior members of the Council. They're right here in New York, sequestered inside a mansion. It's the first break we've had in months."

"That is good news," Penny said. "But don't you find that strange. All known members have been on the run since the incident in Thessaloniki. Why are they here?"

Wisdom shook his head. "I don't know. Not yet. I should have news tomorrow." He clasped his hands together and placed them before him on the table. "You all know how much I detest politics. I've never wanted a seat at the table. Now, I have no choice. I know most of you don't trust me. You're probably right not to, but let me be very clear. The world is at a tipping point. One wrong move and it's a disaster we won't come back from. So I will learn what the Council of Peacocks is planning. Failure, as they say, is not an option."

Chapter Two

Josh Wilkinson sat on the bathroom floor, eyes locked on a half-empty bottle of vodka. Hands shaking with rage, he used his telekinesis to pull the bottle closer. He drank a mouthful and then hurled the bottle toward the shower wall. An instant later, he recovered and, using his power, caught the bottle midair. He punched himself in his bare chest, hoping the physical pain would stop the hollow ache in his chest. He wiped his eyes dry with the back of his hand and set the bottle down before him.

"Why do I keep doing this?" He ran his hands through his shaggy blond hair and stared at the ceiling. "Mom would kill me if she saw me like this." He laughed, the sharp sound turning into a sob. "Course she can't do that. Because she's dead. She's dead and it's all my fault."

There was a knock at the door.

Josh groaned. "Go away, Garnet. I'm fine." He concentrated on the mirror over the sink. The medicine cabinet swung open. A bottle of Prozac flew through the air. It landed in Josh's outstretched hand."

"Please, Josh, open the door." Her voice was soft and close to the wood separated them. "I know you're not okay. I'm psychic, remember? This has gone on long enough. You need to talk to someone."

"I did. Wisdom made me see that shrink on the fifth floor. All I do is talk about it. First to the police, then my uncle. After that, I spent hours with those useless creeps from Candleworks. My mother's dead. My father killed her. And he left a note for me in her blood." He hung his head and closed his eyes. "How exactly is talking about it going to help?"

"Maybe you talked to the wrong people. Open the door. Let me try. If it doesn't help, I promise I won't ask again."

Josh stared at the door handle and held his breath, thinking. Then he shook his head. "The only thing that's going to help is getting my father. I have to kill him. Kill my own father. He has to pay for what he's done."

"I'm sorry, Josh. I know you hate when I say that, but I am. No one should have to go through this. I know what your mother meant to you. You'll get your chance, but we have to find him first. Wisdom has…"

"Wisdom has done nothing." Josh clenched his fist. The bathroom mirror cracked.

"Josh, your TK is out of control. Stop or you'll set off the alarm."

"Fine. But you know I'm right. He's sold off most of his businesses. Hasn't been to our training sessions in months. He even missed Jessica's birthday. All he does is sit in that office and stare out the window."

"That's not true. He has meetings every day. The UN Security Council, Candleworks, the CIA. It might not look like it but he is working."

"Yeah, right. When was the last time you saw him?"

Garnet cleared her throat. "That's beside the point. Look, Wisdom's been through a lot, too. Echo's dead. He traveled back in time, which I can't believe is even possible, and he still lost her. They spent thousands of years together. I don't know if anyone can recover from that. Even Wisdom."

"Then how can I?" He reached for the vodka again, hands trembling. "He lost his girlfriend almost four months ago. I lost my mother three days ago. Weird saying, isn't it? I lost her. Like I misplaced my keys. I didn't lose her. Somebody stole her." A lump formed in his throat and his tongue felt numb. For a moment, he couldn't speak. He wiped his eyes again and swallowed. "I'm so angry. I just want to…stab something. But I can't.

All things considered, I think I'm keeping my crap together better than Wisdom."

"Wisdom isn't drinking himself to sleep every night. He also isn't popping pills he wasn't prescribed. Where exactly did you get the Prozac?"

"Jesus!" Josh punched the wall behind him. The drywall cracked. "Stay the hell out of my head!"

Garnet pounded the door. "Enough! I'm done babying you, Josh. I'll stay out of your head if you open this door. You can't flake out on us, not with Wisdom being the way he is. We need you." Her voice grew quiet. "I need you."

Josh leaned his head back and took a long, deep breath. He looked at the door handle and the lock popped open. It swung open easily, revealing the woman on the other side.

Garnet's straight brown hair was held back in a loose ponytail, framing a face that looked years older than when he had met her only a few months ago. She wore his Arcade Fire t-shirt and a pair of pajama bottoms.

Josh smiled. "Hi there."

"Hey," she said back. She knelt down and brushed the hair from his eyes. Leaning in closer, she cradled his head in her small hands and kissed him on the lips. Josh wrapped his arms around her waist. Pulling her close, he sobbed openly in her arms.

When she pulled back, Josh smiled up at her. "Am I ever getting that shirt back?"

"Never." Garnet stood and, lowering a hand, helped Josh to his feet. "Leave the vodka, okay? Just for tonight."

Josh nodded and followed her out of the bathroom. They walked past his bedroom into the living room. Floor to ceiling windows looked out onto Central Park far below. It was early evening. All the lights in the condo were on. The TV played in the background, unwatched. Two glasses of red wine stood beside an open bottle on the coffee table. "This is supposed to help me with my drinking problem?"

Garnet took one of the glasses and curled up on the couch, pulling her bare feet beneath her. "First off, I never said you had a drinking problem. Secondly, as far as I'm concerned, drinking wine is never a problem. So I'll start by asking the most ridiculous question ever. How are you?"

Josh sat on the other end of the couch and took the other glass of wine. "Never better. Obviously." He touched her leg. The contact made him feel a little less alone. "This has been the worst year of my life. First, serial killers kidnapped me and killed my best friend. They tortured Jan, my girlfriend at the time. Then evil reptilians showed up. Wisdom rescued me, whisking me away to London where I was subsequently attacked by a demon. And that's the easy stuff. Then I found out my father belongs to a secret cult of sorcerers trying to take over the planet. And, to top it all off, I found out he wasn't even my real father. My real father is a creature of darkness named Ehpslab who wears a maggot suit and lives in a hell dimension. And, because of that, I have supernatural powers...which I have to admit is occasionally pretty cool."

"Agreed."

"It sounds ridiculous when I say it aloud. I think the only thing keeping me sane is being here. With you, everyone. No one back home would understand. And there's Elaine. I have to see her every day at self-defense class. She shot my mom once. I know it was an accident but...it's harder to forget that now that my mom's..."

Garnet winced and sipped her wine. "I suppose it would be. I remember those things. I was with you for most of it. And your story's not any crazier than mine." She bit her lower lip for a moment and placed her feet in front of her. "Okay, well maybe a little crazier, but I was a teenage cat burglar. That's got to count for something."

Josh reached over and started massaging Garnet's feet. "Not really a competition. But if it was, I'd win. Amnesia. Alien planet. Trained to be a spy."

"Don't exaggerate." Garnet moaned in pleasure at the foot massage.

"Okay. Trained by a spy. Close enough." Josh grinned and looked away. "How do you do it? How do you sleep at night knowing there are demons out there?"

Garnet shivered. "I've known about the demons longer than you have. I've had more time to…assimilate. You don't have to worry about the Orpheans here. The building is protected."

"That didn't stop Defksquar from getting in months ago."

Then she pulled Josh's hands away and looked him in the eye.

"Tell me the other part, Josh. Tell me the hard part."

Josh felt his eye twitch. He stared at his wine but did not pick up the glass. "The last time I saw my mom I told her I couldn't stay. Not in Ottawa. I said I had to go with Wisdom, track down my father before he hurt anyone else. After all these months, we're still no further ahead at stopping the Council of Peacocks."

Garnet shrugged. "Well, I wouldn't say that. We destroyed the headquarters in Thessaloniki. Hundreds of Council members were imprisoned by Candleworks. We confiscated the technology they used to turn Anomalies into monsters."

"But we lost the other Anomalies. There are still dozens missing. And almost all the upper members of the Council escaped. Including my father." Josh stared at the TV. It was a news report about the strange killings in Ohio last month. It had been all over the headlines for weeks now. The main suspect, Tadgh Dooley, had disappeared. He pointed at the TV. "How does anyone disappear nowadays? This guy is just like my dad. It's like he's on another planet or something. Seriously, with all Wisdom's resources, how has my father escaped?"

"Your father has his own resources. And an army."

Josh crossed his arms, avoiding Garnet's eyes. "I know. The problem is my mom didn't. I don't think she ever knew how dangerous Dad really is."

Garnet reached out, placing a comforting hand on his knee. For a moment, neither said anything.

Josh reached for the wine, drinking the glass in one gulp. "I think the worst part is knowing this won't stop me. I'll get over this. Move on. Everyone loses their parents sometime. This doesn't make me special. It's tragic and horrible. Sad. But I know she wouldn't want to see me like this. Not over her. She'd smack me upside the head, tell me to stop fussing. But I don't want to. The minute I stop…well, that's when I admit she's really gone. She won't see the rest of my life. My wedding. Children. I see her smile, hear her laugh, and I know it's all gone. And I've got to move on. How can I be so cold? Distant. Do you think it's because I'm half-demon?"

"Nonsense." Garnet reached over and stroked his cheek. "You are far from cold, Josh Wilkinson. You feel everything so deeply. It's one of the things I love about you."

"Oh, we're doing the love thing now? Is that something we're doing now?"

Garnet stuck her tongue out at him. "Fine. Yes. I love you. And you don't have to say it. I know you love me, too. Psychic, remember?"

Josh pulled her close and they kissed.

After many moments, Garnet slid back on the couch, her hand tousling his hair. "You try so hard to keep it all in. You've been in survival mode ever since the car crash in the Laurentians. Every day you wake up ready for the next disaster. But nothing could prepare you for what your father did. Nothing could have stopped it, either."

"You're wrong." Josh clenched his fists. "I could have, if I'd been there."

Garnet grabbed his hands, forcing his fists to unclench. "I don't know that. Maybe you could have stopped him. If he came alone. But what if he brought a squadron of Edimmu with him? Or worse. You've seen the reports. The Council has put several Anomalies through the process of Eyeness. They're real monsters now and we have no idea how many survived the turn. You saw the videos. You know what they're capable of. You're strong, Josh. Probably the most powerful Anomaly I've met. But not even you could take on those creatures. Not by yourself."

Josh threw his arm over the back of the couch and waited for the tension to drain from him. When he felt composed again, he spoke. "You're right. I know that logically. But there has to be something we could have done. We could have brought my mother here, kept her safe. That's what we should have done. We knew my father might come back. We left her there. I left her there. As bait."

"No, Josh. You didn't. We all thought your father was done with her. His cover as government agent was blown. Candleworks was looking for him just like we were. There was no reason for him to go back there."

"Obviously there was. He went back there to draw me out. And it worked. He knew there was only one thing he could do to hurt me more than he already had."

"At least we have your other friends under surveillance now," Garnet said. "Jan and the others are as safe as they can be. If he comes for them, we'll know."

Josh nodded but did not look relieved. "You saw what he wrote on the wall. What he wrote with her blood."

"Yes." Garnet placed a hand over her stomach and her face paled.

"Two words. Your fault. Bastard. The Council still needs me for their plans. I'm the one Defksquar needs to bring the device to Earth and activate it. My father couldn't get to me past Wisdom's defenses. So it's all my fault. If I stayed with him, let the Council use me, my mom would still be alive."

Garnet grabbed the edge of the couch, her face red with anger. "Maybe. But the rest of the world could be enslaved. From what you've told me of your mom, she wouldn't want that. You're not the bad guy here, Josh. You didn't do anything wrong."

"And yet my mom's still dead." Josh stood up from the couch and went to the window. He looked out over the park. The sun was fully set. The city was much darker now. "I think you're right, Garnet. I haven't been talking to the right people. I need to talk some sense into Wisdom. He needs to pull his crap together. He's grieved Echo long enough. For months, the Council of Peacocks has hidden from us. Grown stronger. No more. It's past time we wiped them out for good before it's too late."

Chapter Three

Travis Froese had the distinct feeling he was being watched. He stood silent, keys in hand, beside his truck and looked up and down the street. A light frost covered parked cars. Yesterday's snow had melted. Perhaps it would not be a white Christmas after all. Across the street, a large orange cat with bright green eyes stared at him. Otherwise, he was alone.

He looked down at his hands. They were shaking.

'Pull it together, idiot,' he thought. 'What the hell is wrong with me? I've felt this way for months. Like there's this…presence in the shadows. Watching me. Last night I thought there was something under my bed. If this keeps up I'm going to have to see someone. It already ruined my relationship with Cynthia.'

Across the street, the cat jumped off the porch and disappeared.

Travis blinked. Hard. He tried to see where the cat had gone but there was no sign of it.

'I'm cracking up.' He slapped his face. "Wake up. Maybe I'm just weirded out by what happened to Aunt Therese.'

Four days ago, his father's sister, Therese Wilkinson, was found brutally murdered in her Ottawa home. The primary suspect was her husband, Richard. Missing for months, witnesses placed him at the house the day before her body was found. Their son, Josh, was also unaccounted for, presumed dead. On top of that, Travis had had the most horrible dream last night. None of the images made sense: three dark mountains that were not really mountains, a gray-haired man with a gold ring, and something that looked like a giant spark plug.

He unlocked his car, then froze. A pinprick of light flashed for a moment just inside a nearby open garage. For a moment, he stared at it. Then he shook his head and got in the car, immediately locking it.

Still, as he drove to work, he repeatedly glanced in the rearview mirror to make sure he wasn't being followed.

For the last six months, Essex Seafood had been his second home. He'd dropped out of college because he couldn't afford the tuition. It was the beginning of a series of disappointments. His parents divorced. His relationship with Cynthia ended. And now the best job he could find was delivering seafood.

His boss, Arnold Ross, was a petty tyrant: a cruel, hunched-over jerk with hairy arms and beady black eyes. He barked commands and had a tendency to throw large boxes of shrimp when his employees didn't move fast enough.

Barry, one of the few long-term employees, reminded Travis of Burl Ives. He was an eighth-grade dropout and one of the smartest men Travis knew. Every day, Barry told Travis to get out while he still could.

'That's the problem,' Travis thought as he walked up the front steps. 'I can't get out. Windsor's economy is the worst in the country. All the good factory work went to China. I need this job or I'll lose my house."

He opened the warehouse's front door. A clipboard smashed into his face.

"You're late!"

"What?" Eyes watering, Travis fumbled for the clipboard and glanced at his watch. He was five minutes early. Nothing in the world would make him say that to the boss. Arnold stood before him, a slightly more humanoid version of Jabba the Hutt in a striped polo shirt.

"Get in the truck," Arnold said. "Barry's off sick and we have a delivery due five minutes ago. Well, what are you waiting for? Go, go, go!"

Travis mumbled a response and rushed past Arnold.

The truck, of course, was not loaded. He went to the main freezer to get what he needed.

One by one, he loaded ice-covered boxes of fish into the freezer truck. Fifteen minutes later, he closed the back door on the truck and started to leave.

He stopped.

He sniffed twice and turned slowly around.

"What the hell?" For a moment, the thick, strong scent of pine trees and damp earth replaced the stench of the warehouse. As quickly as it hit him, the smell dissipated. The speed it disappeared was just as disconcerting as how quickly it came.

'Smells don't do that,' he thought. 'Smells linger.'

"Maybe it's a brain tumor," he mumbled as he stepped up behind the driver's wheel. "That would be my luck."

Only it wasn't really a brain tumor. Travis was about to find out just how bad his luck really was.

****

On the western edge of the Varnya Rhine, on the planet Maghe Sihre, two nervous soldiers watched the sky. Their sweat-stained uniforms were torn and soiled from weeks in the woods. Yesterday, there had been 30 men in their party. Now only four. Cutting across the nearby plains would get them home faster but they dared not risk it. Open air meant they would be visible to the wypera riders.

"How long has Sir Overyl been gone?" Dairic asked. He was a typical Norshire man: muscular with long blond hair and blue eyes. As a member of the Norshire Salvagers, Dairic was an experienced soldier. A holy warrior, Dairic dedicated his life to the protection of his people.

His brother, Milyan, looked back at the dark woods. He sighed, shook his head, and then continued to clean his sword.

"How long's he been like that?" Dairic stared at the grey-haired man who sat beneath a nearby tree. Gaysun Defksquar, chief geognost to Sir Overyl of Norshire, had been sitting in the same position ever since they set camp. Dressed in a bright green tunic and tanned leather pantaloons, he seemed to melt into the trees. A gold ring on Defksquar's right hand gleamed unnaturally bright.

Milyan shrugged.

"What do you think he's doing?" Dairic asked

"Praying," Milyan said. "You know geognosts. Creepy tree worshippers. Probably communing with pebbles or listening to the dirt. Let him be. If we didn't shake the wypera riders, prayer may be the only thing we have left."

"Not the only thing," Dairic said.

Milyan glanced at the large leather backpack they were transporting back to Norshire. "I have no patience for this sorcery business. You ask me, that stuff is pure evil. We should ship it off to the devils first chance we get."

"For the hundredth time, it's not sorcery. It's no more magic than a wheel or one of those Nizarian laser pistols. It's just a bunch of tools. They were created by the Beherskers, yes, but tools none the less."

"Men don't die for tools, Dairic." Milyan looked up again. Both moons were waning. This far from any large city, stars filled the sky. "My guess, this must have something to do with the war efforts. You've heard the rumors. Demons appearing in the south. Troops movements in the west. Something big is happening. I don't think Sir Overyl has told us the whole story."

***

Gaysun Defksquar snapped back quickly into his body. 'Somehow the boy sensed me,' he thought. 'That shouldn't be possible. The boy has no power. My field manipulation was weak. Only a fieldbender or geognost should have sensed anything.'

"You alright there, Defksquar?" Milyan smiled under his beard. "You look even more pale than normal."

Defksquar raised an eyebrow. "You do realize I could turn your bones into little fangs that would eat you up from the inside out, don't you? Not that I would, but you might want to keep that in mind when you talk to me. And as for Sir Overyl, he told you everything you need to know. Stop acting like a bunch of frightened boys. Remember, you are warriors. You disgrace the men who fell today."

"We disgrace no one, geognost." Milyan spat at the fire and tightened the grip on his sword. "They were my men, not yours. I lost 23 men today for this bag of relics. We deserve to know why."

Defksquar's gold ring twinkled in the reflected firelight. "You don't really care about the Miscellany. That bag of relics is worth more than all our lives. If the Quadruplex gets their hands on it, more than 20 men are going to die."

Defksquar walked to the edge of the gorge and looked at the turbulent white water 50' below. This was part of the Shukton River, a tributary of the Varnya Rhine. He could follow it all the way to Castle Falls where the most crucial part of his plan would be carried out.

"What were you doing under that tree anyway, Geognost?" Dairic walked over to Defksquar and handed him a loaf of dry bread.

Defksquar closed his eyes. "Reconnaissance."

Dairic frowned. "Everything okay?"

"Nothing to be concerned with." Defksquar tore off a piece of bread and ate it. "Nothing I can't handle."

Milyan sheathed his sword. "Ah, the mighty Defksquar, hero of legends. I'd be surprised if you admitted there was anything you couldn't handle. You may be older than the hills and, if the stories are true, you danced with gods, but remember, you're still mortal."

Defksquar flinched and looked down at his left arm. Although the scars were hidden by his long sleeves, he was always aware of them. From the elbow down, the arm was artificial. Aside from a slight difference in color, it looked like natural flesh. Instead, it was advanced Nizarian cybernetics. Tiny gears and wires had replaced flesh and bone. He'd lost the arm in the last Great War. Even two hundred years later, the place where man ended and machine began still itched.

"I can handle this," he said to Milyan. "The plan proceeds."

Sir Overyl ran out of the woods, hands pressed against his stomach. He stumbled and fell to the ground. Defksquar knelt beside him.

"I need to see." Defksquar pulled Sir Overyl's hands away, revealing a jagged wound. "Good news is there's no poison. Hold on, old friend. This should only take a moment."

Drawing power from the magnetic subweb of the planet, Defksquar healed the wound. Muscle and flesh knit together. The bleeding stopped. The pain slid from Sir Overyl's face.

"What happened?" Defksquar stood and lowered a hand to help Sir Overyl back to his feet.

"Bad news, my friend. We didn't lose them." Sir Overyl straightened his uniform. "The wypera are less than five miles to the west."

"Damn it." Defksquar clenched his fists and swallowed his rage. "The Verdenstab gives off a specific energy signal. They knew you didn't have it. They let you get away, hoping you would lead them to it."

Sir Overyl nodded. "I assume so. Have a little faith in me. I still know a few tricks. I bought us some time but I don't think it's enough."

"You want to split up, don't you?" Defksquar lifted the knapsack containing the Verdenstab onto his shoulders. He lingered on the Overyl's reddish brown eyes – a rarity among the clans of the Norshire – the bleached-bone white of his hair and the olive skin covered with scars and wrinkles.

"Unless you can think of another way to throw them off our track. We can't let them get the Verdenstab. What I do is for my people."

Defksquar nodded and clasped his friend's shoulders. For a moment, he found it difficult to speak. Tears came into his eyes.

"I've never been much of a seer but I don't think we will see each other again. Take care and stick to the trees. I've warped your bio-field quite a bit but it won't fool the sharp eyes of the wypera if they catch a glimpse of you. Still, you should be fine unless they have Umbral Knights with them."

Sir Overyl smirked, a twinkle appearing in his dark eyes. "We are Salvagers, Defksquar. We're far from helpless. If Umbral knights they send, Umbral Knights we'll deal with."

"Of course you will," Defksquar lied. And, from the way the light faded in the old soldier's eyes, Overyl knew he lied. "I didn't plan to move so quickly but I can't risk waiting any more. I'll make contact with the boy from Earth today. You know what has to be done."

Sir Overyl looked back at his remaining men. "Yes. Take the slow way. I'll lead them away from you no matter what the cost. I'll see you in the next life, my friend."

Without another word, Defksquar altered his own bio-field, removing it from the gravitational field of the planet. He floated across the gorge, leaving the others behind. It had been many years since he'd felt the pang of loss, but it crashed into him now. But never once did he doubt he was doing the right thing.

Chapter Four

Wisdom had traveled back in time to the late Stone Age. From the edge of the forest, he watched Echo and her sister laughing on the banks of a river. They played in the water, splashing it at each other's faces. Both wore dresses of woven flax, dyed bright blue, Echo's favorite color. Echo's brown hair fell loose over her shoulders. Wisdom had never seen her happier.

'This is before I ruined her life,' he thought. 'Three months from now I steal Echo's life away. Not Echo. She called herself Andromeda in this time. The reason she's so happy is that she hasn't met me yet.' Fury erupted inside him. Flickers of flame danced in his eyes. He stared at the snow-topped mountains in the distance. 'I saw your beauty and I tried to claim it. I was a monster.'

Echo filled a wooden bucket with water and walked with her sister, hand in hand, back to their house. At the front door, her mother took the bucket and scolded the girls for getting all wet. Echo smiled and kissed her mother on the cheek, unrepentant. She tousled her sister's wet hair and went inside.

'When I escaped the Kaz, it took me months to adapt to life on Earth. My body was different. Not quite a djinn but close. Then I realized how strong I was. Powerful. After centuries of being a slave, I became the one with all the power. And I abused it. In the end, I was no better than the djinn. I gathered a horde of bandits. Took everything I wanted. After the monks drove us out of China, we headed west. This village lay in our path of destruction. I burned this place to the ground. Killed her parents and gave her sister to the horde. She never forgave me. I can't blame her. Some things are beyond pardon.'

Wisdom stared at Echo's house for several minutes in case she came back out. Eventually, he sighed and turned away.

'Time to go back to reality.' An oval portal of light appeared beside him, the teleportation disk that allowed him to travel across time and space. He stepped through it, arriving back in the 21st century. He emerged in his penthouse office overlooking Central Park in Manhattan. Outside, an early morning blizzard buried the city.

He was surprised to find Elaine waiting for him. She stood, arms crossed, with her back to the window, dressed for combat: Kevlar vest under black military fatigues. The expression on her face was one of anger. The look in her eyes was one of worry.

"You went to see her again, didn't you?"

"Are we going to do this again?" Wisdom closed the portal and sat on the edge of his desk.

"Apparently." Elaine walked towards him. "You can't keep going back to see her, Wisdom. It's not healthy. Echo died four months ago."

Wisdom's eyes flashed with fire. The room grew hotter. "I'm well aware of that. I was there. She was the love of my life, Elaine. And I've had a very long life." The fire in his eyes dimmed and he put his head in his hands. "I couldn't save her. No matter how hard I tried to change the past, I couldn't stop her from dying. I...don't do well with feeling powerless. At least this way I can see her from time to time."

Elaine lowered her eyes. Her voice deepened. "You visit her every day, Wisdom."

"You don't know that."

Elaine laughed, humorlessly. "Right. It's not like I'm your head of security or anything. It's my job to know. Yesterday you disappeared for three hours. You missed a board of directors meeting. Even though you've divested yourself of most of your holdings, you still have obligations. To your business and the Anom-alies."

Wisdom held up his hands in surrender. "I know, I know. I've heard all the logical arguments. Moving on has proved harder than expected. I loved her so much. She spent centuries hating me. And she was justified. I rewrote history for her. I finally had to admit there were some things even I couldn't control. I promise, I won't go back to see her again."

A condescending smile formed on Elaine's face.

"Ugh!" Wisdom smacked the desk lightly and stood. "I said I promise, okay? Take me at my word. Has Ms. Ryerson returned yet?"

"No." Elaine glanced at her watch. "She should have been here 30 minutes ago. That's why I came looking for you. How long did you spend this time? An hour? Two?"

Wisdom sighed. "Leave it alone. Please. What's the situation with Josh?"

"He's talking today," Elaine said. "Which is an improvement. Understandably, he's taking his mother's death very hard. Garnet gives me regular updates. As you can imagine, Josh is not confiding in me."

"Well, you did shoot his mother."

Elaine grunted. "Just a little bit. That was years ago and I was acting under your orders. Why doesn't he hate you?"

Wisdom smiled. "Well, I'm a pretty likable guy."

"I'm sure I could find several people who would disagree with that." Elaine walked back to the window and looked out at the storm. "Josh's uncle is arranging the funeral. He flew to Ottawa from Windsor yesterday. Josh wants to attend but he understands why he has to stay hidden."

Wisdom went to stand beside her. "I can't believe Richard Wilkinson slipped past us."

"He slipped past Candleworks, too." Elaine rubbed the back of her neck. "I'm still not comfortable working with them. They spent years trying to kill you. Are you sure we can trust them?"

Wisdom shook his head. "I trust no one. Especially secret government organizations. But Jeanette needed protection and Candleworks wants Richard Wilkinson caught just as much as we do. They also have just as much to lose as us if the Council's plans progress any further."

There was a knock at the door.

"Good," Elaine said. "That should be Ms. Ryerson now."

Wisdom turned, frowning. "No. It's not her. It's Josh. I can feel the sadness and rage pouring off him. Why don't you leave us? I think he wants to talk in private."

Elaine nodded and placed a comforting hand on Wisdom's shoulder. She walked out of the room. Josh entered, hands buried in the front pockets of his jeans. He looked over his shoulder, waiting until Elaine shut the door behind him before speaking.

"I need you to snap out of it," Josh said.

Wisdom did a double take. For a moment, he was too surprised to speak. "Wait. You're telling ME to snap out of it?"

"Yes." Josh's face grew hard and emotionless. "We need to move against the Council of Peacocks now. Stop moping and be a leader. "

Wisdom laughed. "Wow. First off, consider yourself lucky I don't backhand you for talking to me like that."

"Oh, please. The tough guy thing doesn't scare me. Besides, I know you need me." Josh walked closer to Wisdom. "You don't fool me, Wisdom. I know you're a good guy, no matter how hard you try to act like a hard ass."

Wisdom scratched his forehead. "I'm pretty sure I don't meet the qualifications for a good guy. But thank you. I think." He left the window and sat behind the large glass desk where he did most of his work. "Now, let's try this conversation again but this time don't be a jerk. Remember, even good guys have tempers."

Josh bit his thumbnail and took a deep breath. "Okay. I want my father dead. I need your help to do that. We've waited long enough. It's time for us to go after the rest of the Council of Peacocks. We know where they are and…"

"Correction," Wisdom said. "We know where MOST of them are. Several dozen of the top leaders have gathered here in Manhattan, but we have zero evidence your father is here. There's also been no sign of Defksquar. But that you know. Despite what you may think, Josh, I have been working. I have regular meetings with the U.N. and Candleworks as well as a few other organizations you don't know about. We all agree on one thing. The facts don't add up. There's something else at work here. I don't want to make a move before I know what that is."

"By then it may be too late." Josh sat in one of the thick leather chairs across the desk from Wisdom. "I left my life in Ottawa to join you for a reason. For the last few months you've had us Anomalies training like crazy. I now have almost full control over my telekinesis. Last week David used his fire power to fly across the room. And then there's Todd. He's trained so hard with the wushu instructors that he's dropped 20 lbs. We're ready. It's time for us to do something."

Wisdom folded his hands in his lap. "I heard of Mr. Ross' accomplishment. Jessica told me he's more annoying than ever because now he thinks he's the Human Torch."

Josh smiled. "He may have said 'Flame On' once or twice."

Wisdom pushed himself away from the desk and stood, smoothing out the folds of his suit. "I know you've all been training, but be realistic. You've only been here for a few months. A few months ago, David had so little control over his power he accidentally set a paperboy on fire."

"I remember. It's why he left Nova Scotia. He's wanted for murder there. But you've seen how much he's grown. He almost never whines anymore."

Wisdom smirked. "Really? Not in my experience. As for Jessica, she's only a child."

"Don't let her hear you say that."

"My point is…you're not ready. Not for what comes next." Wisdom hesitated a moment and looked at the back wall. "I'm going to show you something. Something the other Anomalies haven't seen, not even Garnet. Come with me."

He walked towards the back of his office, stopping in front of a bookshelf. He lifted one of the books and pressed a button hidden behind it. The bookshelf slid away, revealing another room. Black and white photos of council members and crime scenes were fastened with thumbtacks to corkboards on two of the four walls. File folders covered a table in the middle of the room. Wisdom walked past this to the back wall. Dozens of framed photos lined the area. He motioned for Josh to look at one of them, a black and white photo of thirteen men in suits standing on a beach. One of the men was Wisdom.

"Who are they? Friends of yours?"

Wisdom shook his head. "I wouldn't use that word. I'm sure you wouldn't recognize their names. The one on my left is Roscoe H. Hillenkoetter, first director of the CIA. On the right is Dr. Vannevar Bush. He worked on the Manhattan Project. I'm showing you this picture because I need you to realize that I'm very careful choosing my battles. This was back in 1947. The group came to be known as the Majestic 12."

"That sounds vaguely familiar."

"You may have heard the name on The *X-Files*. President Truman brought us together. Once, this group was as big a secret as Candleworks. Not so much anymore."

"Are they still around?"

"The group? Yes. But the members have changed. I'm not in contact with them anymore. They wanted my help with a national security issue. I said no."

"Which issue?"

"Can't you guess? This was taken a few days before the crash at Roswell."

Josh lowered his head and turned slowly to look at Wisdom. "You're kidding."

Wisdom shook his head. "I once told you I made a decision long ago. I could either focus on the Council of Peacocks or the aliens. But not both. I chose the fight I thought I could win. I still think we can win this fight, Josh, but we have to be smart. Rushing in before we're ready will get people killed. Yes, you've been training. And while you trained, the Council has been turning the other anomalies into monsters. They captured dozens under my care and found many more from around the world. We have no idea how many survived the process or what their abilities are. I won't risk your lives by sending you into a battle I don't know we'll win. We've lost enough already."

Josh sighed and looked away. Then his eyes fell on another picture. "Hey! Is that really you with Grace Kelly?"

"That is one story I will not be telling you." Wisdom put a hand on Josh's shoulder and pulled him away from the wall of pictures. "Now, Ms. Ryerson is doing some reconnaissance for us. I assure you, as soon as we know what we're walking into, we'll make our move."

They left the secret room and Wisdom closed it behind them. Then, a figure burst into Wisdom's office. She was a big-boned woman who moved with more speed and agility than her body would suggest. She was the palest person Josh had ever seen - her skin nearly ice-white. She wore blackened and tattered clothes and cradled her right arm with her left. The look on her face was one of pure terror.

Wisdom looked her up and down and saw patches of blood on her clothes. "What happened, Ms. Ryerson?"

"We don't have much time, Wisdom." Her voice cracked with intensity. "The Activation is planned for tomorrow."

Chapter Five

Travis dropped off the delivery and headed back to the warehouse. Waiting at a traffic light, he saw a homeless man talking to the empty spot on a park bench. Travis shook his head and whistled.

'Whatever problems, I'm not that far gone,' he thought. 'At least not yet.'

He shook the thought away. "I'm not crazy. I may be talking to myself and feel like someone's watching me all the time but my paranoia is just because my life is so screwed up right now. Right?"

The light turned green and Travis turned a corner.

***

A wave of pain hit Defksquar. He stumbled and fell into the underbrush. Thorns scratched his skin and tugged at his hair. Pulling himself free of the bramble, he closed his eyes and listened to the talk of the trees.

'Damn,' he thought. 'They caught Sir Overyl. That happened faster than expected.'

The trees sent him images of wypera – large fire-breathing reptiles – and the black-armored creatures who rode them. They dropped from the sky as Sir Overyl left the cover of the woods.

'Looks like they're still alive, but that actually makes things worse. Once they realize Sir Overyl doesn't have the Verdenstab, they'll take them to the Mordant Room of Castle Dispayre. They'll torture him and the others, turn them into Umbral Knights. Sir Overyl is as good as dead. But I'm not. The mission has to continue.'

He pushed himself to his feet and continued down the steep wooded hillside. 'I can do this. I survived imprisonment on my homeworld, the pain of the violent deportation, and the empty fall through space to this desperate world. I even survived losing all the powers I struggled so hard to acquire. If there's one thing that's stayed true about me, it's my drive to do whatever needs to be done.'

When he reached level ground, he opened the backpack and looked inside. A powerful fieldbender, Elmontrazar, had crafted the backpack specifically for this mission. Fieldbenders were experts at manipulation of reality on a subatomic level. This backpack opened to a small pocket dimension, allowing Defksquar to carry the relics easily. Each item was a remnant of the days before the current civilization, an age when the Ancient Ones, the Beherskers, ruled the land. Collectively, the items were known as the Miscellany, but only one item mattered: the Verdenstab.

Millions of years ago, the Beherskers landed on a barbaric, untamed planet. They named it Magohé Shi'Hiar, now bastardized as Maghe Sihre. Most translated Magohé Shi'Hiar as 'Land Crafted by Strong Will'. And that, in essence, was how the world was made: by the will of the Beherskers.

Defksquar stepped into a calm, green clearing, taking in the freshness of the damp air. A waterfall filled most of the elevated horizon.

'Castle Falls,' he thought. 'Legend says this is the spot where the Beherskers stood when they created the world. I never believed the stories. After seeing the Verdenstab, I'm not so sure. True or not, something unleashed a great power here at some point. It damaged the esoteric walls that maintain reality, leaving them weak. Porous.'

The entire area was a giant foramen – an opening in the bones of the planet. Those trained in manipulating the magnetic subweb could use it to travel around the world. Or to other worlds.

'Almost time to make contact.' Defksquar walked to the edge of the water. The river at the base of the waterfall ran southeast to the Varnya Rhine. He stripped and sank beneath the waves, allowing the cool water to erase the stench of travel from his skin. When he was satisfied he was clean, Defksquar climbed out of the river. He dressed and sat cross-legged on the riverbank.

He reached across the worlds and made contact with Travis Froese.

***

Travis was halfway through the turn when the pain hit him. Slivers of ice jabbed through his eyes and lodged in his brain. His nose bled and his body jerked stiffly. Witnesses observed none of this. All they saw was the accident.

His foot slammed against the gas pedal but Travis was barely aware of it. The delivery truck tore into a small Prius, barely slowing. Then it punched through the window of an Ethiopian restaurant.

Travis grunted as the steering wheel slammed into his ribcage. He could not open his eyes. Pain and blindness overwhelmed him.

Then nothingness.

***

Defksquar jerked back to his body. He fell to the damp soil. He crawled forward and vomited in the grass. He experienced only a fraction of the boy's pain. It was still the worst pain Defksquar had experienced since he lost his arm.

He washed his face in the river. 'I know what that was. Interference. That must be how the boy sensed me before. Someone doesn't want me talking to him. Which means they know what I plan to do.'

Chapter Six

Josh watched as Wisdom led Ms. Ryerson to a couch at the far end of the office. He handed her a glass filled with ice and a splash of scotch. She waved the drink away but he forced it into her hands. She took a sip, smiled and stared at the ground.

Wisdom turned to face Josh. "Perhaps you should leave us."

"No," Ms. Ryerson said. She took another sip of scotch. "He needs to hear this. It's about his cousin."

"What the hell are you talking about?" Josh rushed over to Ms. Ryerson and knelt down before her. "Which cousin? I thought you said this was about the Activation. None of my cousins know anything about the Council of Peacocks."

"No, they don't. But they know about him." Ms. Ryerson placed her drink on a nearby table and turned to look up at Wisdom. "We've been so stupid, Wisdom. They've been playing us all along."

Wisdom sat down on the couch beside her. "With each passing day I find my chosen name more and more ironic. Why don't you start at the beginning? What happened at the mansion today?"

Ms. Ryerson took a deep breath and brushed a strand of hair from her face. "Surveillance started normally. I was in the corner of a lounge on the second floor when Lucius walked in. At first, I thought he was alone. Then he stood in front of a mirror. It fogged over from the other side and I heard a voice."

"Wait a minute," Josh said. "You were in the corner of the room and Lucius didn't see you?"

"Of course not," she said. "I was invisible."

"You were…" Josh looked back and forth between Wisdom and Ms. Ryerson. "She can do that?"

Ms. Ryerson rolled her eyes. "Anyway, as I was saying, the mirror fogged over. A moment later, a hand brushed away the fog from inside the mirror. A dark figure appeared. He said, and I quote, 'Defksquar is making contact with the boy today.'"

Wisdom groaned. "I knew we hadn't heard the last of him."

"My first thought was they were talking about you, Josh." Ms. Ryerson turned to face him. "We all thought Defksquar's plan was to use you. Now I know differently. This was never about you. You were never anything more than a distraction."

Wisdom closed his eyes. "Of course. It makes perfect sense now. After this I am officially changing my name. I don't deserve to be called Wisdom anymore."

Josh got back to his feet and started pacing. "I have zero idea what you guys are talking about. That creep Defksquar played with my head for years. Now you're telling me it was for nothing? Which boy were they talking about?"

"Your cousin," Wisdom said. "They were speaking about Travis, right?"

Josh stopped pacing. "What? You're telling me Travis is an Anomaly, too?"

Wisdom shook his head. "No. He's human. It's a brilliant move, actually. Because of your powers, I focused so intently on you I never saw the other pawn on the chessboard. You're safely protected here. Travis is completely vulnerable. And as for your father…" Wisdom let his head fly back and stared at the ceiling. "Damn it. That's why he did it."

"That's why he did what?" Josh clenched his fists. "Tell me."

Ms. Ryerson spoke with a trembling voice, unable to look Josh in the eyes. "They wanted your cousin alone, vulnerable. They needed a reason to isolate him. They drove you further into hiding and created a situation where all Travis' family would have to leave the city."

Realization slammed into Josh's chest like a sledgehammer. He opened his mouth but nothing came out. He turned away, covering his mouth as nausea overtook him. No one said anything until he'd recovered. He took his hand away from his face and turned to face Ms. Ryerson.

"My father…killed my mother…just to get my aunt and uncle out of the city?" Hot tears filled his eyes. "Is that what you're saying? My mother's death was just another distraction?"

Wisdom cleared his throat. "It would have worked, too, if it wasn't for Ms. Ryerson. So tell us, Amelia, what happened next? We need to hear the rest of the conversation."

"Lucius called the creature behind the mirror Ehpslab."

Josh groaned. "Well this just gets better and better."

"You know him?" Now it was Ms. Ryerson's turn to look bewildered. "Who is he?"

"My father." Josh laughed, his voice cracking with the hint of a sob. "The other one. He's the demon that possessed my human father to impregnate my mother. It's because of him that I'm the monster I am today."

Wisdom folded his hands in his lap. "This is obviously not a coincidence. Please, Ms. Ryerson, continue."

"Anyway," she said, "Ehpslab said Defksquar is about to lure Travis over to the other world, whatever world Defksquar is from. I didn't recognize the name at first. Then I remembered an incident from Josh's file."

"Oh," Josh said. "That." Years ago, Defksquar had lured Josh and his cousin through a dimensional rift to a planet called Maghe Sihre. He spoke in veiled threats about Josh being a liability. Weeks before, Josh had interfered with one of the Council's initiatives. He had killed several Edimmu trying to protect one of his childhood friends, Tommy Delonki. The Council had not been pleased. They had convinced Defksquar to intervene. He'd used a gold ring that had magically erased Josh's memory for years.

"I'm afraid so," she said. "Then Lucius said Richard Wilkinson would be happy to know his plan worked. Ehpslab said he would pass the message along."

"Oh dear," Wisdom said.

Ms. Ryerson nodded. "You understand what that means. Richard Wilkinson is within the Black Sea. Somehow he's found a way to be physically inside the dimensional prison of the Orpheans. That's why we haven't been able to find him. But it gets worse."

Josh laughed. "Is that even possible?"

"I'm afraid so," Ms. Ryerson said. "Like I said, the Activation is planned for tomorrow. As we speak, Defksquar is pulling Travis to his world. He will be given something called a Verdenstab, whatever that is."

Wisdom frowned. "It must be the device he told me about. It's a terra-forming device that can alter the physical reality of a planet. When I tracked him down months ago, he told me it could be used to reshape the world in the image of the person who activated it. We have to get to Travis immediately. Defksquar is a master of mind control. The poor boy may have no idea what he's actually doing. I'll gather the others and get to Windsor immediately."

"I'm afraid you can't," Ms. Ryerson said. "As I said, there's worse news. The reason Richard Wilkinson is inside the Black Sea. They are launching a dual-pronged attack. According to Ehpslab, Richard Wilkinson is leading an army to a spot where the walls of their prison have been weakened. He said it would be symbolic. He chose the place where the Black Sea was created. Do you know where that is?"

Wisdom nodded. "We had a different name for it once. Now it's called Gobekli Tepe. It's an ancient ruin recently rediscovered in Southern Turkey. It's over 10,000 years old and should never have been unearthed."

"That sounds familiar, too," Josh said. "Another *X-Files* thing?"

Wisdom smirked. "Not quite. Maybe the Discovery Channel. It's nothing more than ruins now. But at one point it was a highly sophisticated settlement. Many people who survived the destruction of Atlantis took refuge there. When they decided to banish the Orpheans, Atlantean scientists created a pocket dimension in the heart of the city. Then they buried it. For millennia it stayed buried. Recently, archeologists discovered it and began excavating."

"Wait." Josh held his head. "That's way too much information. First off, you're telling me Atlantis really existed? That was a real thing? And how exactly do you know so much about it? And what do you mean by 'the others?' Are there more people like you?" Josh sat on the floor. "I think I need drugs. Lots of drugs."

Ms. Ryerson leaned over and touched Wisdom on the shoulder. "You forget, my friend. Not everyone knows where you come from. One thing I can tell you, Josh, is there is no one like Wisdom. I believe he's referring to the group popularly call the Illuminati."

Josh scowled. "You're not helping! Come on. Seriously? The Illuminati?"

Wisdom waved the question away. "I've always hated that name. And it's hardly the most pressing issue right now. We need to stop that invasion and we need to stop

Josh's cousin from activating that device. The problem is we can't be in two places at once, a quandary I'm all too familiar with." He chewed on his lower lip for a moment then bowed his head "We'll have to split up."

"My thoughts exactly," Ms. Ryerson said. "We can send a small team to Windsor while the rest of us head to Gobekli Tepe."

"I'm actually thinking of three teams." Wisdom rose from the couch and went to his desk. Picking up the phone, he dialed a number. "Yes, Shirley, I need you to get me something. No, it's not another box of Turtles. This is no time for chocolate. I need to arrange a video conference with the heads of Candleworks. Tell them it's an End Game Scenario. That should let them know how serious it is." Wisdom fell silent for a moment. "I am not being testy." He listened for a few moments longer before loudly sighing. "Okay, fine, you can send in the Turtles. But make that phone call first."

He hung up the phone and turned to face Josh. "It appears you were right, Josh. I do need to snap out of it. And for that I'm going to need your help. Ms. Ryerson is right. We have to fight this thing on several fronts. That's why I'm sending Elaine and a group of Anomalies to Windsor to help your cousin. Ms. Ryerson will join Candleworks at invading Gobekli Tepe and stop the invasion from this side."

Josh groaned. "I know I'm going to regret asking this, but what about me? What do you want me to do?"

"First, I have to meet with Candleworks. Then keep the U.N. in the loop. Bloody bureaucracy. That will take a few hours. That's why I hate asking for help. After that, we'll gather the other Anomalies and fill them in. Josh, I know you want to protect your cousin, but I need you to come with me. We're going to follow your father. That means inside the Black Sea."

Chapter Seven

When Travis opened his eyes, the pain hit him. It was less than expected but still intense.

A familiar face drifted into view: a dark-skinned man with classic Italian features and overly-gelled brown hair. Ignatio was one of his oldest friends. They'd met in high school on the volleyball team and stayed close since graduation.

"Iggy?" he said. "Where am I?" He pushed himself up. Pain. Fire and ice. He touched his head and felt bandages. Bandages. He looked down and saw sterile white sheets. An IV stuck out of his right arm. A splint secured his left arm. "What happened to me?"

Iggy shook his head. "Man, you are so stupidly lucky. Doctors' didn't think you'd wake up so quickly. You look like hell, by the way. I'd pass you a mirror so you could see yourself but it isn't pretty. Best guess is you had a stroke. I didn't get much out of them. Had to lie and say I was your husband to get that much out of them."

"Seriously? You told them you were my husband?"

Ignatio shrugged. "I didn't think they would believe brother. Relax, it's not like I had to kiss you or anything. It wasn't like you had anyone else coming for you. I called both your parents. Neither answered their phones.

Travis sighed. "They're out of town planning my aunt's funeral. How long have I been out? Why are you looking at me like that?" He touched his face, feeling for stubble. "Oh, God. Was I in a coma? Have I missed months? Years?"

Ignatio laughed. "Okay, drama queen. Relax. This isn't a TV movie of the week. You've only been out for an hour. See?" He held out his smartphone, showing Travis it was only 8:30.

"Just an hour? Damn." Travis touched his head. "I thought strokes were something only old people got."

"You realize you're leaving yourself wide open there."

Travis laughed then touched his ribs. "Ow. That hurt. I did feel weird this morning. There was this weird smell. That's common with strokes, right?"

Ignatio tilted his head downwards. "You're seriously asking me for medical advice? I work in a tool and die shop. What do I know about strokes? Anyway, sorry to be the one to tell you, but you're going to have to find a new job. My uncle had a stroke and they took away his license for months. Depending on how the tests go, you may get it back eventually. But you won't be driving anytime soon."

"Fan-freakin'-tastic." Travis lay back down in bed. "God. I remember now. There was an accident. Was anyone hurt?"

Ignatio nodded. "Yeah. You totaled a car. I heard the people inside got whiplash. You also ran straight into a building, which is going to destroy your car insurance. On the plus side, I hear public transit is good for the environment."

"I'm going to be sick." Travis turned away and stared at the wall.

Ignatio patted Travis' forearm in comfort. "Just be grateful you didn't kill anyone. It's a miracle, if you ask me. I'm going to let the nurses know you're awake. Don't go anywhere."

"Funny," Travis said. After Ignatio left, he closed his eyes and tried not to cry. Just one moment and his life was completely altered. What the hell was he going to do now?

***

In the shadows beneath a chair in Travis' room, two inhuman creatures waited.

"Carla, I know we've had this conversation before, but are you sure we've got the right one?"

Silence.

"I said…"

"I heard what you said," Carla interrupted. "I'm just tired of answering you. We have the right man. Defksquar reached out to him. You felt that."

"Yeah, but…"

"Remember why we're here and why we disrupted the communication."

"I know, but he just looks so…"

"Pathetic?"

"Yeah."

Carla's voice lowered. "Well, trust me. He won't look pathetic for long."

***

Travis stared at the clump of shadows under a nearby chair. For a moment - just a moment - he could have sworn he'd seen a pair of glowing eyes clearly showing in the darkness. Then they were gone. He convinced himself it was just the medication and closed his eyes.

***

Defksquar paced at the edge of the river. Although tired from hours on the run, he was too wound up to rest.

"I can't feel Travis anymore. Something broke our connection. If he's dead, do I try the plan with Josh? He's protected by the djinn-spawn, Wisdom. Worse, his biosphere is tainted with Orphean energy. There's no way to know how that will alter the Activation."

He crossed his arms across the chest and turned to face the foramen, the weak spot in the dimensional fields that connected Earth to Maghe Sihre.

"There's another option. I can head to Earth and find another human. That's a risk. Their genetic makeup could be defective. And as soon as I cross over, the Quadumvirate will sense it. They could cross over to

Earth, too. And the humans are not prepared for that battle."

A trickle of energy hit him.

He exhaled loudly and collapsed on the ground. "Thank the gods. Travis is awake. I have to get to him. We haven't spoken since he was a teenager but the time for subtlety is over. I don't know who it was but it's clear someone attacked him. I need to get him to cross the foramen and pick up the Miscellany before they stop him for good."

Chapter Eight

Six people sat around a mahogany desk waiting for Wisdom to arrive. Josh sat at the far end, closest to the windows. The storm raged outside; the wind rattled the glass.

Ms. Ryerson sat on his right, still in her torn clothes. Garnet sat to his left wearing a crisp green pant suit. Todd sat next to her, barely recognizable as the same man Josh met four months ago. After rigorous daily training, Todd had dropped much of his flab, replacing it with well-defined muscle. His brown hair was cut short. He wore loose black khakis and a tight white t-shirt that emphasized his chest. There was also a cold steeliness to his expression that had not been there before.

"Come on," Garnet said. "Give us a hint. What's this about?"

Josh shook his head. "Wait."

Todd grunted. "I hate waiting. I thought Wisdom was done with all this keeping secrets stuff."

"He is," Josh said. "Just…I need him to tell you what's going on. You won't believe it coming from me."

"Pretty sure I'll believe just about anything now," Todd said. "A few months ago we fought winged reptilians in the secret lair of evil sorcerers allied with demons. Nothing's going to shock me after that."

Josh thought back to his earlier conversation with Wisdom. "Don't count on it."

Todd turned to the thirteen-year-old girl who sat to Ms. Ryerson's right. "Jessica, can you get anything from Wisdom?"

Jessica pulled on her pony tail. "Stop asking me! I told you I don't read Wisdom's mind." Jessica looked around at everyone at the table, shoulders pressed back, a look of defiance on her face. "Okay, maybe that one time I did, but I promised him I would never do it again. And I won't. "

"You realize no one believes you," said the twenty-something man sitting on Jessica's other side. This was David Ross, native of Dartmouth, Nova Scotia and would-be Human Torch. He wore a blue blazer over a white cotton dress shirt. His red hair and freckles hinted at his Scottish heritage. "Just tell us what you saw. Be a team player."

"Don't lecture me, David Ross." Jessica said. "I'm more a team player than you'll ever be. Just because you stopped whining every time Wisdom asks you to do something..."

"I don't whine. Excuse me if I freaked out because we were attacked by an army of winged reptilians. That makes me sane, not a whiner."

"Whatever. You're the king of whiners. Baby wanna bottle?"

"Stop it. Both of you." Ms. Ryerson glanced at her watch and then checked her cell phone. "We can't afford either of you acting like children. Not anymore. It's time you learn to act like adults."

Jessica opened her mouth to respond. Ms. Ryerson raised her eyebrow. Jessica fell silent.

Everyone turned as the door opened. Wisdom came in, followed by Elaine. They both quickly sat down at the table.

"Sorry to keep you waiting," Wisdom said. "I spent the last 30 minutes on a video call with Abdullah Gül, the prime minister of Turkey. I wanted to get his permission before going ahead with the plans."

"What plans?" Todd leaned forward.

Wisdom cleared his throat. "You mean Josh didn't tell you?"

Everyone turned to look at Josh.

Josh threw up his hands. "Hey! Don't look at me. I'm going to leave this one to the professionals."

Josh sat back as Wisdom told the others in the room about Ms. Ryerson's reconnaissance mission and what she had uncovered about the Council's plans. Fifteen minutes later, the room fell silent as everyone drank in the news.

Todd leaned back and put his hands behind his head. "Is this a stand up fight, sir, or another bug hunt?"

Josh groaned. "It's bad enough you made me watch that movie. Do you have to quote Starship Troopers every day?"

"A day without Bill Paxton is a day not worth living," Todd said.

David scratched his jaw. "So…we're invading Turkey?"

"Don't be stupid." Jessica threw a pen at David. The pen bounced off his chest. "Of course we're not invading Turkey." Then she turned to face Wisdom. "We're not, are we?"

Wisdom shook his head. "The only one in this room staying in Turkey is Ms. Ryerson. I have other plans for the rest of you. I'm forming two teams. One will go with me, the other with Elaine. Her group will head to Windsor to track down Josh's cousin Travis. We have his address but he could be anywhere by now. Jessica, you're the strongest telepath we have. Find him. David, I know your powers have grown, but approach Defksquar with caution. He is a dangerous man. Both of you remember, Elaine's in charge. She doesn't have your abilities but she is an experienced soldier. She'll keep you alive."

Elaine walked around the table, giving each person a folder filled with color photos. "This is your target, Travis Froese. He's 22, 6'2" and 205 lbs according to his last physical. He lives alone, drives a Ford F-150. Sandy brown hair, blue eyes. As you can tell, there's only a slight physical resemblance between Travis and Josh."

Josh looked at the picture of his cousin and felt something in his gut grow numb. A few months ago, Josh's entire world had been shattered, rebuilt into something he barely recognized. Sadly, the same thing was about to happen to Travis.

Wisdom leaned forward. "Your only goal is to stop Defksquar from activating that device, no matter what the cost. Try not to kill Travis unless you have to."

"Gee," Josh said. "Thanks. So gracious."

Wisdom's eyes flared. "Look, I know he's your cousin, but what he's about to do will destroy the world as we know it. We don't have time for sentimentality. Josh, Garnet and Todd, you will come with me into the Black Sea."

Todd slumped in his seat. "I think I'd prefer going to Windsor."

Wisdom frowned. "I won't lie to you. The Black Sea is a dangerous place. A pocket dimension filled with demons who have been cut off from humanity for thousands of years. As soon as you use your abilities, they'll sense it. As for the group heading to Windsor, we have no idea if Defksquar will be there. We still have no real understanding of his motivation or power levels. We also don't know if he's working alone. Our hope is that the Council of Peacocks is focusing their forces at Gobekli Tepe. I've seen what the Orpheans are capable of. I hope the army is enough to stop them from spreading across Europe."

"Is there any good news?" David slumped down in his seat. Then, as if realizing what he'd done, he forced himself back to an upright position.

Wisdom smiled, weakly. "Not so much. As far as we know, Richard Wilkinson is the only human who has ever physically entered the Axeinus and returned. Both Josh and I have been there in a dream state but we have very little intel on it. We don't know how many Orpheans exist, what their power levels are like. Hell, we don't even have accurate information on how big the place is. All we know for certain is that it's a pocket dimension filled with homicidal monsters with immense psionic powers."

"You mean our parents," Josh said.

Todd inhaled sharply. "Damn. Don't call them that."

"But that's what they are," Josh said. "The only reason we exist is because of those creatures. Orpheans possessed our earth parents, using their bodies to create us. All our powers come from them."

Wisdom shook his head. "That may be true, but you can't think of them as your parents. I promise you, they don't think of you as their children. Most would not even recognize you. The only one who has ever reached out to any of his procreations is the Ehpslab. For some reason he has reached out to Josh. That's another reason I want Josh in the Axeinus with me. We'll be leaving in a few minutes. Say your goodbyes. Who knows when or if we will see each other again."

Chapter Nine

Josh stepped out of the teleportation disk and stood beside Todd, Garnet, and Ms. Ryerson. In the west, the sun was setting, the sky filled with orange and red clouds. Back in New York, it was just past 9:00 in the morning. Here it was almost 6:00 in the evening.

Heavy shadows obscured much of the surrounding scenery. Dozens of stone pillars and excavated stone circles filled with stone ruins. In the distance, electric lights lit row after row of tents. Hundreds of soldiers walked around the area, assault weapons in hand. The largest concentration of soldiers stood in front of a massive T-shaped stone at least 20' tall.

"What is this place?" Josh turned in a circle. The ruins spread out in all directions.

Wisdom stepped out of the teleportation disk. With a wave of his hand, he closed it behind him. "Gobekli Tepe. Older than Stonehenge and much larger. The sections they've found so far date back 9,000 years. Thankfully, they haven't found the older areas yet." He pointed left towards a small path worn into the rock floor. "That's where you're heading, Ms. Ryerson. Be careful in the dark." He pulled out a plastic card from his pocket and passed it to Ms. Ryerson. "Show this to General Ozel. He's expecting you."

"What is it?" she asked.

"Security codes for the Turkish military databases. Tell him we'll publish the information on the web if he gets too mouthy. He has a problem with women in authority."

Ms. Ryerson pocketed the card. "I'm sure Ozel will be fine. We discussed gender politics and my right hook the last time we worked together." She leaned forward, embracing Wisdom briefly. "Don't get yourself killed, old friend."

Josh watched her walk down the rocky path towards the soldiers. The night wind picked up, driving a chill into his bones.

"This place is massive," Todd said.

Garnet shrugged. "It's not as impressive as I expected. The pictures were way more interesting."

Josh turned to her. "Pictures? What pictures?"

Garnet held up her smartphone.

"You Googled it?" Josh shook his head. "When did you have time to Google Gobekli Tepe?"

Smiling, Garnet put her phone away.

"I take it we're not following her?" Garnet rubbed her arms, chilled.

Wisdom pointed to the north. "No. We're going there. They haven't unearthed the section we need yet. Thankfully." He raised his left hand. Fire leapt up between his fingers, creating an odd sort of light. While not as bright as a flashlight, it seemed to banish the darkness better. "Follow me."

Todd was the first to follow Wisdom. "If they haven't dug it up, how are we getting in? Teleporting?"

"Not quite," Wisdom said. "I have control over all the elements, not just fire. I'll move the earth out of our way. It may be safer for everyone to have an escape route in case I'm otherwise occupied."

Garnet grabbed Josh's hand and walked side by side with him down the gentle incline. "You're okay with this?"

Josh's eyes went wide. "Are you kidding? I'm so not okay with this. There is nothing about this situation that any sane person would be okay with. But what choice do we have?"

Garnet squeezed his hand, slightly. "When this is over, why don't we get away for a bit? Just you and me. Have you ever been to Banff?"

Josh shook his head.

"It's gorgeous this time of year," Garnet said. "With any luck we could be there by Christmas."

"Really?" Josh frowned. "You know, I have absolutely no concept of time any more. The last few days have been a complete blur. I guess I forgot Christmas was so close. What day is it?"

Garnet looked to the east. "When the sun rises here tomorrow, it will be December 17."

Up ahead, Wisdom stopped suddenly. "Dear Lord. It all makes sense."

"Come again?" Todd scratched his chin. "I think you lost me there."

Wisdom started walking again. "I'll explain later. We don't have much time."

Ten minutes later, they stopped at a section of greenery. Short grass extended in all directions beneath a series of trees Josh could not identify. He looked above, momentarily stunned by the beauty of the night sky.

"I had no idea there were that many stars," he said to Garnet.

"My father was an amateur astronomer." Garnet's eyes brightened, a small smile on her lips. "He taught me the constellations as a kid. Over there, near the horizon, that's Orion. Above us, that really long one is the sea serpent. Almost directly above us is the Lion. Everything looks so different from this part of the world. Same shapes but slightly different locations. You know, I've never traveled very much. Funny the things you think about when you're facing sudden death."

"Don't say that," Josh said.

"Why not? It's true. I know what we're doing is important. I get that. I wish there was more time for us. We've only just started to…"

Josh kissed her on the lips to silence her. When he pulled away, he touched her lightly on the shoulder. "You're right. We've just started. Don't write our eulogies yet. You're the strongest person I've ever met. Maybe you've forgotten that, but I haven't. I may need you to save my butt in there. Keep your head in the game, okay?"

Garnet smiled. "Fine. It's a beautiful butt to watch."

Wisdom cleared his throat. "If you're finished with your scene from *Twilight*, I'm ready to reveal the entrance."

Josh felt blood rush to his head. Embarrassed, he pulled away from Garnet.

Wisdom raised his hands, palms stretched out towards the trees. He flicked both wrists and the earth cracked open. Clumps of dirt and grass flew into the air, creating mounds of earth on either side of the newly-created entrance. Josh stood behind Wisdom and looked into the opening.

"Holy!" Todd clapped his hands. "Do it again. Better yet, teach me how to do that. Please?"

Wisdom lowered his hands. "Sure, Todd. Right after we save the world. Now stop being such a fanboy and stay focused." He bent down and picked up a dead branch from one of the nearby trees. He handed it to Garnet. "Can you be a dear and help with the light?"

Garnet sighed, taking the branch. "Fine. You know I hate using fire." The top erupted in flames. "I still don't understand why we didn't bring flashlights. This is the 21st century, you know. All of our cellphones have flashlights in them."

"We can't rely on technology. It doesn't work the same in all dimensions. The flashlight app could function properly. Or the electric current inside your cellphone could start a nuclear event. I'm not willing to take the risk."

They stopped at a large stone door.

"What language is this?" Josh studied the pillars on either side of the door. They were covered in pictures and symbols Josh could not understand.

"Atlantean," Wisdom answered. "Well, one of the dialects. I haven't read it in centuries. Can't make out most of it but I do understand this part." He touched a symbol like an upside down house and the stone door swung open. "That means enter."

"So let me get this straight," Todd said. "You expect us to believe you're centuries old and that Atlantis really existed?"

"And he dated Grace Kelly," Josh said. "I saw the pictures."

Wisdom smacked Josh lightly on the shoulder. "Tattletale. We did not date. And it was only one picture. Focus."

Josh looked at Todd. "They totally dated."

Wisdom groaned. "I told you after Thessaloniki, no more secrets. But with everything happening, I haven't had time to tell you my whole life story. I was born in Atlantis a long time ago, many years before it sank. But there are more pertinent topics than my biography. Let's get inside."

Garnet stepped into the doorway. Light from her torch flickered over sand-colored bricks and a stone-grey floor. Josh followed, noticing that the floor consistently sloped downwards. The single hallway led to a small circular room. A raised dais stood in the middle of the room. Two square pillars rose to the ceiling: one black, the other white.

But it was the object at the back of the room that Josh could not take his eyes from.

"Are you kidding me?" Todd raced past Garnet and stood beside a pyramid of jet black glass illuminated from the inside by small green lights. "It looks like something from Star Trek."

"It's a computer," Wisdom said. "A very specific type of computer. It interacts with the pillars and the platform to manipulate dimensional barriers. I've seen them in operation but I'm not sure of the actual science behind it. They were common when I was a child, used mostly to created links between power generators and the sun. In principle it functions very much like my teleportation disks. If you enter the correct code, you could, in theory, use this device to create a doorway between this room and anywhere in the universe."

"So, it's a *Stargate*," Todd said.

Wisdom winced. "You know how much I hate that show."

"Seriously?" Todd put his hands on his hips. "How can anyone hate Stargate? You know, you kind of look like Teal'c."

A flash of fire flew through the air, racing past Todd's head.

Garnet laughed. "Don't say that again, Todd. I think that's the reason why he hates *Stargate*."

Josh leaned forward to study the glass device. "So if this works like your teleportation disks, why can't you just zap us into the dimension?"

"It's blocked," Wisdom said. "I've been trying to get in since we got back from Thessaloniki. There is some sort of barrier keeping me out. Probably the same thing keeping the Orpheans in. Best not to push the barrier too strongly. This device hasn't been used since the Orpheans were banished to the Axeinus. We just have to reactivate the last coordinates entered and the doorway should open."

"How do you know it hasn't been used since then?" Garnet cocked her head to one side and studied the pillars. "If this device has been tampered with we could end up anywhere."

Wisdom shook his head. "Impossible. I've kept my eye on Gobekli Tepe for centuries. No one has used it for a very long time."

Josh looked around the room. He saw nothing else of significance. "So what did you mean, 'It all makes sense now'?"

"Today is December 17th." Wisdom pushed a series of buttons on the glass device. The pillars on the platform lit up, a series of symbols appearing. "In ancient times it marked the beginning of Saturnalia, a Roman festival that, among other things, celebrated the reversal of roles. Slaves became masters and vice versa. Entire social structures were leveled. It seems the Council of Peacocks is having themselves a little joke."

Garnet nodded slowly. "They see themselves as the slaves who are about to become masters of the world."

"Yes." Wisdom pushed a blue button on the device. When the pillars began to hum, he stepped back. The pillars hummed. "It was also the leadup to the Winter solstice, the longest night of the year. A dark time that also saw the birth of the son of light."

"Sounds like Christmas," Garnet said.

"As it should." Wisdom glanced around the room. "Almost ready. I can see the dimensional strands of this place weakening, twisting. Be ready everyone. We have no way of knowing what we'll find on the other side."

He heard a crackling sound, like electrical charges hitting water. The air between the pillars filled with a shimmering light.

Todd's eyes went wide. "Just like…"

Garnet put a hand over his mouth. "Don't say it."

Wisdom walked towards the pillars. "I'll go first. Be ready for anything."

He stepped into the light and was gone.

Todd pushed himself away from Garnet. "Come on. I can't be the only one to realize this is just like *Stargate*."

Josh smiled and patted Todd on the back. "Only you could geek out at the mouth of hell. If you ask any Orpheans for an autograph, we will leave you behind. Come on. Let's get this over with."

The three of them followed Wisdom into the Axeinus.

Chapter Ten

David Ross stepped through Wisdom's teleportation portal, arriving in Windsor. Jessica and Elaine, who had stepped through the portal before him, stood beside a large oak tree. They stood in a suburban backyard behind a white raised ranch house. Windsor was a nine-hour drive northwest of New York. While Manhattan was in the midst of a blizzard, Windsor was snow-free and sunny.

David took off his gloves and unbuttoned his winter jacket. "I like Windsor already. This is like September weather back home."

"This place sucks." Jessica put her hands on her hips. "Why couldn't we have a mission in Hong Kong or some other civilized place?"

"Speak for yourself." David took a deep breath of the cool air. "Hong Kong was a madhouse."

Elaine also took off her gloves, placing them in her coat pocket. "Count yourself lucky we didn't have to go to Hong Kong. Tracking down Josh's cousin will be much easier here than in a city of seven million. Any sign of our target?"

Jessica touched her right temple and closed her eyes. "He's not here. There's no one inside the house."

Elaine removed her gun from the holster at her hip. "Stay here. I'll do a sweep of the house. Let me know if we get company."

Jessica groaned. "This isn't my first break-in. Just go already."

Elaine picked the lock on the back door and stepped inside.

David looked around the backyard. Dry orange leaves covered the ground. A section of yellowed grass hinted at a recently removed above-ground pool. The fence around the backyard was high enough to hide them from neighbors on either side. Traffic sounds were minimal. A plane flew above, the rumble of its jets muffled by distance.

Nothing visible explained the chill settling in his bones.

"Something's not right here." He walked past Jessica to the latched gate leading to the driveway. The feeling grew stronger. "Can you scan the area? We're not alone."

"Of course we're not alone, idiot." Jessica came to stand beside him. "We're in the middle of a flippin' city. There are three people next door to the right. A middle-aged woman is doing dishes. Her husband is getting ready for work, and their kid is watching cartoons. The house to the left is empty. Across the street some pervert is looking at extremely disturbing images on the internet."

"Keep searching." David unlatched the gate and left the backyard. Sweat built up along the back of his neck. There was no sign of movement, only parked cars with melting frost on the windows. "There's someone else here."

Jessica grabbed him by the arm and spoke with a harsh whisper. "Get back here. We're supposed to be secret-like. Wandering around the front of the house isn't exactly a ninja move, David. Although it's pretty in line with your char-acter."

David knelt down to look Jessica in the eyes. "Can you seriously not feel that? Stop looking for humans. This is…something else."

With an annoyed little sigh, Jessica closed her eyes. A moment later, her eyes shot open, wide and frightened. "What is that? Where is it coming from?"

David shook his head and moved closer to the front of the house. "You're the one with the telepathy. That's not the way my powers work."

"Well, you felt it before I did. Try your psycho-metry."

Jessica's powers were two-fold: telepathy and telekinesis. She could throw a car across a parking lot or read minds from blocks away. While David could do neither of those things, he had his own gifts. Firstly, he was a pyrotechnic. He could psychically generate and manipulate fire. When his powers first manifested, he was only able to start small fires: wood, paper, and clothing. Now he could shoot spears of flame and fly short distances. David also possessed psychometry, the ability to read the history of objects and places by touch. Over the last few months, Ms. Ryerson had trained him, and the others, daily. His control over both abilities was more sophisticated now.

David knelt down and touched the driveway. The instant his fingers touched the concrete, images filled his mind. He saw Josh's cousin, Travis: washing a car in the driveway, unpacking groceries, stumbling home drunk, making out with a girl on the hood of his car. He pushed through all these to find the most recent image.

"I see him. He's getting in a car heading to work. Which, based on the time of day, makes sense. But I see him looking across the street. He feels he's being watched. Damn it. I see them. There are two sets of glowing eyes in the shadows across the street." David took his hand off the driveway. The images in his head faded. "There were two Orpheans here."

Jessica looked around at the shadows. "If they were here before, they're gone now. I know what those things feel like. What I sense now is something different."

A jolt of pain shot through David's head. He closed his eyes, overcome with nausea. When he opened them, he saw an orange cat across the street. Its eyes glowed brightly for a moment. Then it ran behind a tree and disappeared.

Elaine came around the side of the house. "What happened?" She reached for David, helping him stay steady on his feet.

David shook his head. "I have no idea. We felt something."

Jessica frowned and crossed her arms over her chest. "Whatever we sensed, it's gone now. But Elaine, we have an issue. David used his creepy psychometry trick to find out Orpheans were here. They were watching Josh's cousin."

Elaine re-holstered her gun. "We knew the Council was manipulating him. Now we know how. They're using Orpheans. Any sign of that guy with the gold ring?"

David frowned. "Maybe. I suppose that could be what we felt. Anyway, I saw where Travis went. He left for work a few hours ago. Did you find anything inside that could tell us where he works?"

Elaine held up a piece of paper. "Paystub. He works at Essex Seafood. I've got the address."

David frowned. "What we don't have is a car. What should we do? Call a cab?"

Jessica punched David in the stomach. "Will you ever not be an idiot? Hello? Telekinesis. I'm going to steal the car from that pervert across the street."

"You can hot-wire a car?"

"Possibly," Jessica said. "But it's easier to use the flippin' keys. Am I the only one with brains? I've already unlocked his front door. The keys are on a hook in the kitchen."

"I can grab them," Elaine said.

Jessica grinned. "No need. I'm lifting them out as we speak. By the time we get to the car, they'll be on the hood, waiting for us. I also shut down the guy's brain. He'll be asleep for the next few hours. Won't even notice the car is gone."

David shivered. "And you call my powers creepy. I'd hate to see what you could do if you turned evil."

Jessica skipped away. "Silly boy. You're assuming I'm not evil now."

***

Minutes later, they arrived at Essex Seafood. Elaine parked the car, a white mini-van, and turned off the engine.

Jessica touched her temple and closed her eyes again. A moment later she shook her head. "He's not inside."

Elaine inspected the parking lot ahead of them. "I see delivery trucks. He could be a delivery driver off on a run."

Jessica shook her head. "Shh. I'm prying." Her face tense with concentration. "Okay, Travis' boss is a complete asshat. But I found out what happened to Travis. He's in the hospital."

David clenched his fist. "What happened? Did the Orpheans attack him?"

Jessica shrugged. "Can't say for sure. There was an accident. Travis blacked out and crashed his car. His boss is going to fire him if he wakes up. He doesn't seem to think that's guaranteed."

Elaine turned to Jessica. "Can you tell which hospital? I memorized the maps of this city before we left. Get me a name and I'll get us there."

"Wait a sec." Jessica touched her temple again. "Met. They took Travis to Met Hospital."

David bit his thumbnail. "Something doesn't add up here. Jessica, what happened to the truck, the one in the accident?"

"It's just around back. Not much damage to it. They're going to drop it off at the garage later. Look for the one with the broken headlight."

David nodded and got out of the car.

Elaine jumped out. "Where do you think you're going? We have to get to the hospital."

"We also need to find out what happened. I'm going to read the truck. Jessica, let me know if anyone comes outside."

Without waiting for Jessica to respond, David walked towards the truck. Putting his hands in his pockets, he tried to act as nonchalant as possible. Thankfully, no one came out of the warehouse. As he got closer, he heard someone screaming hysterically inside.

'That must be Travis' boss. Jessica is right. He does sound like an asshat.'

There were three delivery trucks in the parking lot. David quickly noticed the one that had been in the accident. The grill and hood were dented, headlights and front window shattered. The sides were marred with scratch marks. David went around to the driver's side and opened the door. As soon as he put his hand on the steering wheel, images flooded his mind again.

He jerked his hand away as icy pain stabbed through his eyes. The pain faded as quickly as it came. He ran for the car, no longer concerned with being nonchalant. He got in the car and slammed the door shut.

"We have a problem," he said. "The Orpheans attacked Travis."

"That doesn't make any sense." Elaine tilted her head to the side and pursed her lips. "They're working with the Council of Peacocks. This whole thing is their plan. Why attack Travis if they want him to activate the device?"

"I think that's the problem." David rubbed his forehead. A dull headache formed behind his eyes. "Maybe we misunderstood the Orpheans' plan. They're trying to stop Travis from activating the device."

Elaine studied David for a moment before starting the car. "They want to activate the device themselves. We have to get to the hospital. If you're right, Travis is still in danger."

Chapter Eleven

As the doctor left his room, Travis turned to face the wall. He threw his right arm over his face, hiding the hot tears that seeped from his eyes. Just like Iggy had predicted, the doctor told him they were suspending his license. It would be several days before he could go home. He could expect all of those days to be spent lying in the uncomfortable bed under thin sheets wearing the ridiculous smock. Travis had never felt so alone. So exposed. So vulnerable.

He closed his eyes. The medication made it difficult to stay awake. Then the strange smell came back to him. Pine and fresh air.

He pushed himself up to look around. He was no longer alone.

At the end of his bed stood a man in a ridiculous costume: bright green tunic and brown leather pants. He also had a gold ring on his right index finger. For some reason, Travis felt mesmerized by it. But the most jarring thing about the man was that he was translucent. Travis saw clear through him.

"We don't have much time," the man said. "I need you to remember me."

The ring flashed. A rush of memories came back to Travis. His head flew back in an unseen wind and the visions came, forcing gusts of memories to swirl around in his head.

***

Years ago, Travis stood next to his father inside the terminal of Windsor's airport. They were waiting for his Aunt Therese and her son, Josh.

Travis looked up from his Nintendo DS. "Do I have to?"

"Yes," his father said. "Be nice to your cousin. It's not going to kill you. He's been through a tough time lately."

"I know. Some kid he knew died. What does that have to do with me? I have a life, you know. You can't expect me to put everything aside to hang out with some loser."

His father grunted and punched Travis lightly in the arm. "Josh is not a loser. He's a good kid. Be nice to him or you can forget about going to that party this weekend."

"So not cool." Travis put his DS away. "Fine. I'll pretend to like the loser. Happy?"

His father crossed his arms. "Ecstatic."

When Aunt Therese and Josh landed, they drove back to the Froese family home. His father and aunt spoke rapidly in the front seat. Travis did his best to ignore Josh. There was something odd about him, a coldness in his eyes that made Travis uncomfortable. Like barely-concealed insanity.

That night, at supper, Travis learned Josh was a runner. After a stern look from his father, Travis invited Josh to go running with him the next morning. They ran to the banks of the Detroit River, then along the parkland paths all the way downtown. Halfway through the 10 km run, most people would have been winded. Josh barely broke a sweat.

They ran together for the next three days. In the silence, they found a connection. A competitiveness. Josh pushed Travis to run faster, further. Travis broke through Josh's shell, dissipating the creepy cold expression in his eyes. By Friday, his father didn't have to pressure Travis to spend time with Josh. He even invited him to Iggy's party.

Most of that party was a blur. Travis drank a few too many beers, had a few too many shots. But one moment remained clear in his memory: a flash of gold light from behind the pool shed. He remembered putting down his drink and walking away from Iggy. As he got closer to the shed, he sensed movement in the shadows. At first, he thought it was an animal. Coyotes were rare in the area but becoming more common. Then he saw him: a man crouching at the edge of the back fence. Darkness concealed his features but the gold ring on his finger glowed mysteriously.

"Get the hell out of here!" Travis clenched his fists.

The man did not move.

"I'm warning you." Travis took a step forward.

The gold ring flashed and the man stood.

"Screw you." Travis leapt at the man, punching at his face.

Then his memory skipped. He couldn't remember what happened next. The next thing Travis knew, he was walking back to the pool, his knuckles scraped and bloodied.

The next day, Travis and the whole family went for a picnic. His father suggested Ojibway Park, the largest wooded area on the west side of the city. Not long after the meal started, Travis saw something shine at the edge of the woods: a glint of gold.

Josh and Travis ran into the woods to confront their stalker but quickly lost track of him.

Travis looked over at Josh and blinked. For just a moment, his cousin looked like a predator. He seemed to grow several inches taller. When he moved, his feet made no sound against the ground.

Travis stared at him. "How did you do that?"

Josh looked confused. "Do what?"

Travis hesitated, then shook his head. "Never mind."

Something caught Travis' attention. "Wait." He put a hand on Josh's shoulder and pointed at a spot several yards away. "Over there."

A shadowy blur moved through the trees. Travis and Josh followed it as it disappeared behind a massive oak. They ran for a bit but Travis fell behind quickly. His cousin, Josh, was running impossibly fast.

"Wait!" he shouted. "Slow down. I can't keep up."

Josh stopped and pointed at the shadow moving ahead. "The thing we're following? It's moving too fast to be…"

"Thing? Too fast to be what?"

"Too fast to be human."

Travis, who was several inches taller and more muscular, stared at him. "I'm guessing you don't mean it's a deer."

Josh shook his head and looked back into the woods. "I think I know what this is. You should go back. It's not safe."

Travis looked down into Josh's eyes. "No way in hell am I heading back without you. When we catch this guy and you see he's nothing but a perverted Peeping Tom, do me a favor and start taking your meds."

Josh smiled. "Deal."

Josh ran more slowly after their target. Travis jogged easily behind him.

"I've never been this deep in the woods before," Travis said. "I had no idea it even went this far. We must be over the Salt Mine by now."

A few seconds later, Josh stopped.

"What is it?" Travis stopped beside him. "Did you lose him?"

Josh shook his head and looked around at the woods. "Where the hell are we?"

Travis turned to look at the trees. They towered above him, larger than any tree he'd seen before. Thick trunks rose all around him.

"This isn't right," he said. "Windsor doesn't have redwoods or any type of tree this massive. What the hell is going on?"

"I don't know," Josh said. "But I'm guessing our friend does."

The further they went, the thicker the underbrush. Eventually, Travis heard something unexpected – a familiar and inexplicable rumble.

"Do you hear that?" he asked.

Josh listened again and nodded. "Yep. That's definitely a waterfall. I think we can safely say we're not in Windsor anymore. Come on. Let's get this over with."

They walked through the strange woods for another ten minutes before reaching the banks of a river. It was easily as large as the Detroit River, several kilometers wide. Unlike the river that ran between Windsor and Detroit, this one glistened a translucent blue. It reminded Travis of the waters along the beachfront in Bermuda. It smelled salty, too.

"Over there." Travis pointed his cousin to one of the most imposing physical landmarks he'd ever seen. Before him, an escarpment covered with foliage shot up over five hundred feet. A section of the greenery gave way to rocks and grassland. It appeared as if the forest there had burned to the ground years ago and was only slowly coming back to life. Above the escarpment, birds with large green beaks and leathery wings circled above the trees. The fact that he could make out their wings and beaks from such a distance suggested they were the size of elephants.

The waterfall ran like a slash of blue and white down the face of the cliff. It slammed into the river below, hiding the base of the escarpment behind a roar of mist and noise. The only thing he could compare it to was Niagara Falls, but he'd never stood in the shadow of anything like this.

Travis rubbed his eyes. "Dude, where the hell are we? Is this Africa?"

Josh blinked. "Africa? Are you on drugs? Does this look like Africa?"

"Well, kinda."

"No! This is not Africa. This isn't anywhere on Earth."

Travis punched Josh in the chest again. "If we're not on Earth, where are we?"

"Maghe Sihre."

The cousins turned as one at the voice, their hands clenched into identical fists. At the edge of the woods stood a strange-looking figure, a tall man with braided gray hair that hung down to the middle of his back. He was pale, with a complexion that could pass for Caucasian until you noticed the green tinge to his flesh. He had vestigial gills along his neck and unnaturally long fingers. But these things were only noticeable if you looked closely. At first glance, he was just a man standing at the edge of the woods.

The stranger took a step forward. Travis flinched. Josh did not.

"I'm afraid there won't be time for introductions," the stranger said. "Not today. You are here because I made a promise, Joshua. Your father is a very powerful creature and he's worried about you. He's concerned about the way you slaughtered his employees."

Now it was Josh's turn to step forward. "My father isn't a powerful man and he definitely doesn't have Edimmu as bodyguards."

"Who exactly do you think your father is?" The stranger smiled. He crossed his arms over his chest, giving Josh the first clear sight of the source of light they'd been following. A simple gold ring on the man's right hand shone brightly even in plain daylight.

"I know exactly who my father is. You have one minute to explain who you are and why you've brought us here."

"And how," Travis added abruptly. "Tell us how you've brought us here."

"Or what?" The man laughed with what sounded like genuine amusement. "Oh my, Joshua. You are so much like your father. Always throwing around meaningless threats. Tell me, do you actually believe I'd let you get close enough to lay a finger on me?"

Thorny vines shot out from the darkness of the woods. They wrapped around Josh's and Travis' wrists. Before either of them could react, the vines lifted them off the ground. The stranger said something to Josh. His voice was too quiet for Travis to make out the words. Then there was a flash of light and a sensation of falling backwards.

Later, Travis woke up in the forest, all memory of the events gone.

***

The rush of memory faded. Travis turned to the stranger. "I remember! What did you do to me? How could I have forgotten that?"

Defksquar looked over his shoulder as if listening for something. "I suggest you keep your voice down. You're the only one who can see me. If the doctors hear you talking to invisible people it will be harder for you to get out. I need you to come back to the woods where we first met."

Travis looked down at himself. "If you haven't noticed, I'm not exactly in travel condition. And why would I do anything you say? You spied on me, attacked me. I don't even know your name." Travis stopped. "Did you kill my aunt?"

Defksquar frowned. "I have no idea what you're talking about. I've never met your aunt. If you get to the woods I can heal you. You're not safe where you are."

"But I'll be safe with you?"

"Safer. My name is Defksquar. I'll explain more when you get there. What happened to you this morning was not an accident. You were attacked. If you don't get out of the hospital, soon they could attack again."

The lights went out.

Travis squealed. Thin streaks of sunlight filtered into the room through the curtains over the window. The shadows seemed to grow.

Defksquar's body was luminescent. He looked more like a ghost than ever. "Damn it. They're here. You have to get out now. I can't help you until you get to the woods. Go quickly!"

From the hallway, someone screamed.

Adrenaline pushed him to move. Ignoring the pain from his ribs and broken arm, he got out of bed and snuck over to the open door. He peeked up and down the hallway. Emergency lights filled the empty corridor with dark red light.

"I have a very bad feeling about this." Travis turned back to look at Defksquar. "I feel like I'm stuck in a horror movie. *Halloween 2*. What's going on?"

Defksquar came forward and spoke in Travis' ear. "I'm trying to give you something that will save your world. Creatures called Orpheans are trying to stop that. They shouldn't be this powerful but somehow they've broken free from the Axeinus. They've already attacked you once today. I can't risk them getting to you again. C'mon. Follow me. We need to get your out of this building. Now."

Defksquar walked into the hallway, his ghostly figure creating a small pool of light in the darkness. Holding his thin hospital gown close to his body, Travis followed.

They didn't get far before the emergency lights faded out as well.

Chapter Twelve

Josh stared forward, eyes wide. "Wisdom, I know you said be ready for anything. I have to tell you, this is not what I expected."

Wisdom said nothing in response. His face was expressionless as his eyes darted around.

The portal had brought them to the top of a cliff overlooking a valley. Behind them were two pillars identical to the ones back in Gobekli Tepe. Josh saw a ragged rock ceiling high above them. He knelt at the edge, studying the highly organized city at the foot of the cliff.

Paved streets in a grid pattern spread in all directions. Two-story stone houses were clumped together in tight neighborhoods. A small pyramid stood in the very center of town. The top gleamed with a black capstone. Tall rock buildings encircled the pyramid, their numerous windows illuminated with soft yellow light. But the strangest part, the thing Josh couldn't process, was the appearance of the inhabitants of the city.

Todd knelt beside Josh. "They look normal. Human. Are we sure this is the right place?"

Josh watched men in black jumpsuits load boxes onto a cart that floated above the ground. From this distance, he couldn't make out their features, but Todd was right. They looked human. Each had brown skin and long, ebony black hair. They reminded Josh of the First Nations tribe in Kahnawake. Mohawks. In another part of the city, a woman stood on the front porch watching a group of children playing in the streets.

Josh stood and turned to Wisdom. "I expected something with a bit more fire and brimstone. Is it possible we ended up somewhere else?"

Wisdom shook his head. "This is the Axeinus. I'm sure of it."

"So where are the demons?" Garnet tossed her torch aside. The ambient light of the city below made it bright enough to see without it.

Todd pointed at the children. "Those people down there look an awful lot like, you know, people. Actual people. What the hell is going on here?"

"Things are not always what they appear to be." Wisdom said. "Whatever you think you see, these people are getting ready to invade Earth."

"Well the children aren't," Todd said.

Wisdom sighed loudly. "Well then I won't kill the children. Now come on. This is obviously not where the army is being amassed. We have to move. There's not much time left."

Garnet pointed to the left. "I think I see a way down. That tunnel is marked with the same symbols we saw on the door earlier. Can you read them, Wisdom?"

Wisdom examined the plaque on the wall to the left of the tunnel opening. "You're right. Atlantean script. This should take us to ground level."

Josh glanced once more at the city below before following Garnet to the tunnel. He couldn't shake the feeling that the situation was more complex than expected.

***

They crept along the outskirts of town, doing their best to stay unseen. Now that they were closer to the inhabitants of the city, Josh saw they did not look much like people after all. They were taller. His best guess at their average height was 10' tall. Although their coloration was similar to Mohawks, many had thick ram-like horns protruding from their foreheads. Others had fluorescent eyes or slender tails. He watched a woman with four arms argue with a group of men in the black jumpsuits. They were too far away to hear the conversation.

Wisdom led them through backyards and alleys lined with garbage. They crossed bridges over streams of black water. When there was no other way forward, they crawled through narrow aqueducts. Thankfully, the water was not deep.

The aqueducts ended abruptly. Wisdom, who led the way, looked over the edge before turning back to speak to the others.

"There's a ladder," he said. "Don't know how far down it goes. Can't see the floor from here. We should take a break before we head down."

"Are you sure we're heading the right way?" Todd seemed to regret asking one second too late. He blushed as Wisdom stared at him.

"He has a point, Wisdom," Garnet said. "There were two ways out of town. Why are we going this way?"

Wisdom narrowed his eyes. "I can sense things you can't. There were no humans or Edimmu in the other direction. I can feel reptilians this way. Trust me. This is where we need to go."

Todd looked back down the aqueduct towards the city. "Are we seriously not going to talk about this?"

Wisdom scowled. "Talk about what?"

Todd stabbed his finger in the air. "About that! This isn't a hell dimension. It's a civilization. They're not all demons. Some of them are just children."

Wisdom sighed loudly. "The Nazis had children too, Todd. Being able to procreate doesn't make you one of the good guys. You know what these creatures have done. Brutalized your parents. Committed countless atrocities across the world for millennia. You've read the files. Seen the videos. So they're not carrying pitchforks and bathing in a sea of flame. Get over it. They're still the enemy and we still have a job to do."

Wisdom climbed over the edge and descended the ladder. One by one, the others followed.

By the time they reached solid ground again, Josh's hands were exhausted. A layer of black dust covered his palms. He wiped them clean on his pants.

They stood in an immense cavern lined with dust-covered statues. Josh looked up at one. It held a black crystal out above his head as if using it to attack the sky. His features were heroic despite the bug-like eyes and horns.

Garnet touched his shoulder. "I hear what you're thinking. You're not alone. We're all thinking it."

Josh frowned. "Well then. maybe it's time someone said it."

Wisdom stood at the feet of another statue: a very human-like man wearing a toga, with a trident in his hand. He had long flowing hair and a beard to match.

"That looks like Poseidon," Josh said.

Wisdom nodded but said nothing.

"Who are these people?" Josh moved between Wisdom and the statue. "I know they're Orpheans, but that's all we know about them. Where did they come from? Why were they imprisoned?"

Wisdom lowered his head. "Tell me this isn't the time you chose for a history lesson."

Todd cleared his throat. "We need to understand, Wisdom. You've always told us to know our enemy. Now we realize we don't know them at all. Besides, we may not get a better time to learn."

"Agreed," Garnet said. "We need our heads in the game, not wondering if the game is wrong."

Wisdom glanced at all three of them, and then shrugged. "Fine. But I'll only talk if you all agree to keep walking. We have a long way to go still." He pointed at an opening behind the Poseidon statue. "We need to go this way."

They followed Wisdom through the opening. Glowing spheres of light lit the pathway. The floor and walls were smooth, giving the area a metallic look.

"It's a long story," Wisdom said. "I'll do my best to tell it quickly. It all started in a town called Peos, back in Atlantis. I wasn't there when it happened. The djinn had captured me by then. A group of scientists developed a means of creating an artificial life form."

"So the Orpheans are robots?" Todd glanced backwards as if he could still see the city.

"No," Wisdom said. "You are. The life form they created is what we now call humans."

Josh stopped mid-step. "No way."

Wisdom waved the comment away. "Do you want to hear the story or not? Believe me or don't. But if you want me to tell you about the Orpheans, you need to stop interrupting every two seconds." Wisdom paused for a moment, looking at each member of his group to ensure they were listening before he continued. "Good. The artificial life forms were a mix of two genetic materials. One was Atlantean. The other was the civilization you now call the Neanderthals. The creation itself wasn't the problem. It was the debate that started the war. You see, some people believed the humans had no soul, no independent intelligence. As such, they could be used for manual labor. Slavery, essentially. Others stayed true to the teachings of the state religion, the Law of One. They believed all living things had a soul. Human, Atlantean, Edimmu, other. The origin of the shell is immaterial. The eternal spirit is all that matters. That comes from the creator."

"What do you mean 'other'?" Todd raced ahead of Wisdom. "Do you mean there are other races?"

Wisdom nodded. "A story for a different day. What you need to know now is the Law of One believed humans had a soul. Others did not."

Josh looked down at his hands. "So you're saying we were all...clones?"

"No," Wisdom said. "I don't believe that. I think the Atlantean scientists created better vessels for souls looking to incarnate on Earth. But that's not what the Sons of Belial believed. They used humans as tools. Nothing more. Like many fundamental disagreements, it eventually led to a war. This one destroyed Atlantis. Many years later, the remnants of the Sons of Belial were rounded up and imprisoned here. Some refer to it as the Pontus Axeinus. Others call it the Black Sea. And here they've stayed for thousands of years."

Todd bit his lip. "So you're saying the Orpheans are the descendents of evil Atlanteans?"

Wisdom winced. "I wouldn't call them that. Their forefathers came from Atlantis but these creatures, these monsters are something else. In the last days of the war, when it looked certain the Sons of Belial would lose, they turned their genetic manipulation skills upon themselves. They injected their soldiers with a pathogen that altered their DNA. It enhanced their telekinetic and telepathic abilities. It also mutated their bodies. Gave them horns, scales, tails. A significant percentage of those treated with the pathogen went insane, prone to acts of mindless rage. Worse, the infection passed onto the next generation of children. In the end, these creatures have a weaker tie to Atlantis than you do."

"Why do they look like First Nations people?"

"Again, a story for another day."

Garnet held up her hand, signaling everyone to be quiet.

Josh turned to ask her what the problem was. But, in the silence, he heard it, too.

The drums of war echoed around them.

Chapter Thirteen

Travis followed Defksquar's specter through the dark hallway towards the stairway. Behind him the darkness intensified. It seemed solid now, like a slow-rushing tide. He heard a wet sound, as if something soaked in blood was being dragged across the floor.

"You'll have to continue on your own for a bit," Defksquar said. "The strain of projecting this far into your world limits how long I can stay."

Travis shook his head. "You leave and so does the light. You expect me to walk down these stairs in the dark?"

Defksquar looked over the side of the railing. "Either that or stay here and wait for the things crawling around in the dark to find you. Keep your hand on the rail. Move slowly. I'll meet you in Ojibway. Hurry."

Defksquar's body faded away. The stairwell plunged into darkness.

"Freaking fantastic." Travis closed his eyes. Somehow that made the darkness more bearable. Somewhere in the distance, a man screamed for help. Then Travis heard the heavy footsteps of someone running, followed by a vicious cougar-like snarl.

'So, going back is not an option. Here we go.'

Keeping his hand on the rail and his body close to the side, he lowered his foot until it hit the next step. One step at a time, he went down three flights of stairs. Then he heard something from the stairwell above. A woman's voice.

"And I'm telling you he went this way, Sanchez."

A deep, male voice responded. "I feel nothing. Just admit you lost the boy, Carla."

"I didn't lose him," the female voice came closer. "The stranger from away is masking his scent. It's faint but I'm sure it's this way. You can go back to killing people or we can find the one we're here for. Which do you think will make Ahriman happy?"

For a second there was silence. Travis held his breath.

"Fine," the male voice said. "Lead on."

'Crap!' Keeping his breath as quiet as possible, Travis moved. His instincts told him to run, but rationally he knew moving too quickly in the dark would be disastrous. He hit the bottom of the stairs. The sudden stop was too much for him. He fell forward, his head bouncing off the floor.

"Did you hear that?" the female voice asked.

In response, the male laughed. It was a bone-chilling sound.

Travis crawled forward. 'The door has to be here somewhere.' His fingers touched cold steel. Getting to his knees, he reached up until he touched the door handle.

"Are you down there, Travis?"

Hearing the strange voice say his name was almost too much for Travis. His heart beat frantically. Getting to his feet, he pushed the door open as silently as possible. He ran through the door and down a dark corridor. The slap of his bare feet against the floor echoed.

'Which way?' He opened his eyes and looked all around. In the absence of light, he saw nothing. 'I have no idea where I am. If I choose the wrong way I could end up deeper within the hospital.'

Ahead, the beam of a flashlight lit up the hallway.

"Over here!" Travis said.

The beam shone on him, momentarily blinding him. Travis covered his eyes.

"It's not safe to be out of your room." The voice was deep but feminine. The light flicked up, illuminating the face and uniform of a female security guard with dark brown skin and short hair. "The power should be back on soon. I'll help you get back to your room."

"Like hell you will," Travis said. "Haven't you heard the screams?"

The guard shined the light back on him. "What floor are you from?"

Travis sighed. "Not the mental ward. I was in car crash. Please, we need to get out of here. Get me somewhere the lights are on."

"Fine," the guard said. "There's a few people gathered in the waiting room. Follow me."

The door behind Travis opened. Two sets of red eyes glowed at waist level.

Travis screamed and ran towards the security guard. The guard shone her flashlight at the open door. Travis caught his first sight of the things following him: creatures of pure shadow, slightly larger than humans. When the beam from the flashlight hit them, both female and male voices howled in pain. It only lasted a moment before the creatures jumped back to the safety of the shadows.

"Jesus save me," the guard said as she crossed herself. "What the hell are they?" she asked as Travis approached.

"Just run!" Travis said. "Run fast."

His bare feet pounded against the hard hospital floor, pain jabbing his ankles and shins. An accomplished runner, he quickly passed the guard. He heard a scream behind him. He looked back in time to see shadowy hands grab the guard by the neck and slam her against the wall. Her flashlight hit the floor, fell, and rotated to dimly illuminate her face. Travis saw her eyes widen in terror. She screamed again. One of the shadowy creatures stuck an arm into the woman's mouth, blocking the scream. Then, inch by inch, it shoved more of itself into her.

"Shit!" Travis said. He turned in circles, unsure which way to run. He knew he couldn't save the guard. Travis didn't want to be there when it fully entered her. He saw a glint of hope: a dim light shone on the wall ahead of him. As he ran towards it, he heard something that sounded distressingly like an animal tearing apart meat, followed by laughter. 'Can't think about that,' he thought. 'Have to keep my mind focused on what's in front of me.'

The light came from a glass door leading to the parking lot. Outside, sunlight covered everything in a bright glow.

'They don't like the light,' he thought. 'I should be safe there.'

Fumbling with the handle, he pulled it open and rushed outside. He found himself at the top of a short flight of concrete steps. A group of nurses and doctors, all in uniform, stood in a clump at the edge of the nearby parking area. Travis ran towards them. Something slammed through the doors behind him. Glass flew everywhere. The doctors and nurses turned towards the sound.

Unable to stop himself, Travis looked back. The guard stood in the doorframe; only he could tell it was no longer her. A black-purple aura covered her body. She stared at him then turned to look over her shoulder as if speaking to someone else. Then, the not-guard jumped, covering 30' in one leap. She landed on one of the fleeing doctors. She grabbed him by the throat and dragged him back to the open door.

'Not safe out here anymore.' Travis focused on the road in front of him. It was Tecumseh, one of the major streets in Windsor. Cars moved in both directions. 'Those things possess people. No way of knowing what else they can do. Time to go. I need to find some place safe.'

Chapter Fourteen

Josh held up his hand and leaned against the rock wall. "Just a second. I need a break."

Wisdom sighed but didn't turn around to face him. "Fine. A quick one. You rest here. I'm going to scout ahead."

His back to the wall, Josh sank to the ground, leaning against the stone. He massaged his sore calf muscles. Garnet came to sit beside him. Todd sat on the opposite side of the tunnel.

Todd looked at his watch, frowning. "Any idea how long we've been walking?"

Josh shook his head. "Feels like hours. I'm exhausted."

Garnet massaged the back of her neck and looked around. "We should have brought water. Food. I never expected this place to be so big."

Josh looked up at her. "How many cities have we passed now? Four? Five?"

The tunnel behind the Poseidon statue had ended at an open-air raised promenade. To Josh, it resembled a set of train tracks running through a mountain range. On either side of the walkway was a thousand foot drop. Below, fields of stone spread to the horizon. He saw no sign of vegetation, only pools of black water. Occasionally, they saw hints of civilization: pyramids, towers, and cities.

"Four," Todd said. "I think the last thing we passed was a shopping center, not a town. The Orpheans are nothing like what I expected."

Garnet nodded. "Agreed. Wisdom said this was a prison dimension. I expected something a bit more…penal."

"We should have known better." Josh leaned his head back against the wall and closed his eyes. "They've been in here for thousands of years. Look at Australia. They were a penal colony once. Look at it now. It was much easier to hate these things when they were just monsters."

"They're still monsters." Todd picked up a rock and threw it down the tunnel. "These bastards killed our friends. Bethany. Amy. They kidnapped the other Anomalies, doing who knows what to them. Maybe the Council of Peacocks did the dirty work, but these Orpheans were just as involved."

Josh nodded. "I guess you're right. It would just be easier to demonize them if they acted a bit more, you know, demony. The one I met before, Ehpslab, he looked like a demon. He had black-gray skin covered in scales and boils. He wore this suit of living maggots and beetles. I expected all Orpheans would look like that."

All three fell silent, wrapped in their own thoughts. Todd broke the silence.

"Do you think he was telling the truth?"

Josh didn't have to ask. He knew Todd was talking about the origin of humans.

Garnet cleared her voice. "I think so. He has nothing to gain by lying to us about it. But it's too big. I can't process that right now. I have to keep my mind on the mission."

"But what if it's true?" Todd clasped his hands together. "Is Darwinism debunked? What does it say about God? I'm sure my pastor back home would say all this is just lies from the devil to tempt us off the righteous path."

Josh raised an eyebrow. "I never figured you for the religious type."

Todd rolled his eyes. "Why? Because you know me so well. No offense, Josh, but do you even know my last name? Where I come from? How many brothers or sisters I have?"

Josh winced. "Your last name's McLaren, but good point. Once we stop the world from being destroyed, we'll sit down for beer and wings. You can tell me your life story."

Todd chuckled and stuck out his hand. "Deal. But you're buying."

Josh shook Todd's hand just as Wisdom returned.

"Break's over," Wisdom said. "I found a path that will get us closer to the military base. It's not far away now."

Chapter Fifteen

Travis was freezing. His feet were scraped and sore from running on cold concrete, but he didn't dare slow down. Other people on the sidewalk gave him a wide berth. He realized he must look crazy, running from a hospital wearing a blue hospital gown and with one arm in a cast.

'Can't afford to panic,' he thought. 'Think. Need to get clothes. Get somewhere safe. Not home. Those things found me here. Might know where I live.'

Ahead, a teenage girl stood at a bus stop talking on a cell phone. As he raced past her, Travis pushed her aside and grabbed her phone.

She shouted something at him as she fell to the ground. Travis ignored her and hung up on whomever she had been talking to. Keeping one eye in front of him, he dialed a number and put the phone to his ear. The number rang once. Twice.

"Come on, come on."

The phone picked up and a familiar voice responded. "Hello?"

"Iggy!" Travis tried not to scream, but his relief nearly overwhelmed him. "I'm in bad trouble, man. I need you to come get me. Now!"

"Hold on," Iggy said. "I just got home from seeing you at the hospital. You haven't had time to get into more trouble."

"Apparently I have. Can't talk now. They're coming after me and…"

"Hold up. Who is coming after you? The police?"

"No!" Travis interrupted. Travis reached the street corner. The light was red. He ran across the street anyway, dodging cars. "Look, everything has gone crazy. I need your help."

A sound like thunder rumbled behind Travis.

"What the hell was that?" Iggy asked.

"I have no frickin' clue. And I don't want to stick around to find out."

"Okay. I'll be there in ten minutes. Where do you want me to pick you up?"

Travis looked around. "I don't know, man. I can't see a good place to hide. I think it's best I keep moving. Meet me by Franco's. I should be there in ten minutes. Oh, and Iggy? Can you bring me some clothes, too?"

Iggy hesitated for a moment. "You owe me an interesting explanation after this. And many, many beers."

'I'll give you an explanation but you already owe me. Remember that incident with the overzealous gymnast?"

"You promised you'd never mention that again."

Travis laughed. "My silence can be bought. See you soon."

He hung up but held onto the phone. From behind him came the sound of metal slamming into metal and car horns. His reflexes forced him to turn around. Three cars had slammed into each other, but it wasn't them that Travis focused on. It was the doctor who had been dragged back into the hospital. Now his body glowed just like the security guard's. Only now, the doctor stood at least 20' tall. The first car must have hit him, knocking him to his hands and knees. Travis opened his mouth to scream but could not find his voice.

The doctor/creature stood and dusted off its thick arms. Then he picked the car up over his head and threw it into a nearby building.

"Crap, crap crap." Travis spun around, running faster than ever.

***

Iggy's car was parked in front of Franco's, motor still running. Travis ran towards it and jumped inside.

"Go!" Travis screamed.

Iggy put the car in drive and sped down Tecumseh. Travis put his seatbelt on as they drove, a difficult act with only one useable hand. Then he stared out the back window. Behind them, more cars were being thrown around. The chaos grew.

"Clothes are in the back," Iggy said. "I thought you were on drugs or something but…" Iggy glanced in the review mirror. "I can't believe the cops aren't here yet. What the hell is going on back there? It's like Godzilla attacking Windsor."

"Everything's a mess. So confusing." Travis ran a hand through his hair. Rubbing sweat from his face, he dried his hand on his hospital gown. "All I know is I was in my room and then people started screaming."

"You said something was chasing you. How do you know they're after you?"

Travis sank into his seat. "Christ. I heard them call my name. Look, I'd tell you more but there's no way you'd believe any of it. I'm not sure I believe it. And I lived it. I need another favor. We need to get to Ojibway Park."

Iggy looked over at him and gave a slow blink. "Because a provincial park is a great place to escape the car-throwing monster. Are you insane?"

Travis bit his thumbnail. "Quite possibly."

After driving for ten minutes, Iggy parked his car in the parking lot of Ojibway Provincial Park. Several cars were parked nearby. The visitor center was filled with tourists.

Iggy turned off the ignition. "Okay, looks like we lost whatever was back there. Can you tell me now what the hell is going on?"

Travis grabbed the clothes from the back seat with his good hand. "Let me get changed first." He stepped out of the car and fumbled his way into the pants. They were a little too large for him but he immediately felt better. Running away from monsters with a bare behind made him feel extra vulnerable. He struggled to put on a t-shirt, poking his good arm through the sleeve. He stepped into the boots and tossed the coat across his shoulders before getting back into the car.

"Okay," he said. "Here's the deal. I'm going to tell you a story. It's one hundred percent true but you're not going to believe a word of it because, despite what I usually tell you, you're a sane and rational human being. But I'm only going to tell if you promise to let me finish the whole thing and don't stop me to ask any questions until I'm done. Okay?"

Iggy scratched his head. "Like I said, there'd better be a lot of beer involved after this."

Travis bit is thumbnail again and took a deep breath. "It all started at a pool party. Remember that time back in high school when I caught some pervert spying on us?"

Iggy nodded.

Travis told him the rest of the story, from the trip to Maghe Sihre with his cousin Travis to his escape from the hospital. When he finished he turned expectantly to Iggy and waited.

Iggy blinked rapidly. "Well, luckily for you I saw all the car tossing. Otherwise I'd be dragging your butt to a psych ward. I don't even know how to process any of that. So why are we here?"

Travis looked out the window. "Like I said, Defksquar told me to come here. He has to give me something."

"Are you sure you want it?"

Travis shook his head. "Not even remotely sure. I want to go back to yesterday but I don't see that happening. Instead, I'm going to head into the woods. The picnic table we sat at is over there. As good a place to start as any. Hopefully, Defksquar will reach out to me again."

"Want me to come with?"

Travis shook his head. "No. Do me a favor and wait by the car. We're in the middle of nowhere. I'll need a ride out when I get back. Something tells me things are just getting started."

Chapter Sixteen

"What the serious hell is that?" David watched the chaos from the church parking lot across the street from the hospital. Two giants with black-purple auras stood in the middle of the street. They picked up nearby cars, tossing them into trees, on top of buildings, or hammering them down on other cars. "They're like 20' tall."

Elaine held her gun at her side. "I've seen this before. Orpheans. They possess human bodies so they can temporarily exist beyond the Black Sea. I saw them attack a village in Africa this way but never in a civilized area. They must be desperate to act this openly."

"We have to stop them," David said. "They're killing all those people."

"Not our mission." Elaine holstered her gun. "We're here for Josh's cousin, Travis, and him alone."

"But…"

"She's right, David." Jessica touched his forearm. "Stopping the Activation is more important."

Reluctantly, David turned away from the giants. The three of them went behind the church to avoid the fleeing people and flying cars.

"These must be the ones tracking Travis," Elaine said. "My guess is he escaped the hospital and they're trying to find him." She turned to Jessica. "Are you getting any reading on him? Is Travis nearby?"

Jessica closed her eyes, then stomped her foot in frustration. "There's too much interference! All I can sense is fear and pain coming from dozens of people. I can't filter through the noise."

A loud crash forced David to turn around again. A Volkswagen had flown over the church, crashing into a nearby house.

Elaine spat on the ground. "We can't stay here. With all these cars flying around, it's only a matter of time before a fuel tank explodes. Let's assume Travis left the hospital. Which way would he go?"

"He could go home," David said. "Unless he knows those things are after him. In that case he'd probably go in the opposite direction. Phone a friend."

"I have something." Jessica pointed west. "There's a girl in that direction thinking about a crazy guy in a hospital gown who stole her phone."

"Great work, Jess." David ruffled her hair which elicited a quick kick in his shins. "Let's head over…"

Before David could finish, something picked him up by the waist and held him high in the air. When he recovered from his shock, he looked down. One of the giants had grabbed him with one hand. Up close, he could see through the dark aura. Behind the energy were the features of an attractive woman with brown skin wearing a security guard uniform.

"Where did you come from?" The giant spoke with a distorted voice, like a voice from a radio station with a weak signal. "Sanchez, look what I found. An Anomaly."

The second shadow figure approached, dragging a station wagon behind. "Don't play with it, Carla. Kill it. You know those things are dangerous."

"But it's so cute." The first giant, Carla, tightened her grip on David. "And little."

"How's this for cute?" David placed his fists on the massive hand gripping his waist and called upon his power. Flames erupted around David's body, half an inch beyond his clothing. Carla yelped, releasing him immediately. As David landed on his feet, he shot a spray of flames at the station wagon the other giant carried. As the ribbons of fire shot through the air, David turned and ran back towards the others.

"Move!" He shouted at Elaine and Jessica.

"Relax, newbie," Jessica said. "I got this."

As soon as David ran past Jessica, she threw up a telekinetic shield. David knelt down behind her and looked over her shoulder. Flames engulfed the station wagon. The second giant, Sanchez, suddenly realized the danger. He turned to throw the car but it was too late. The flame reached the gas tank and the station wagon exploded. Heat and shards of metal flew in all directions. They bounced harmlessly off Jessica's telekinetic shield. Moments later, the flames dissipated. There was no sign of the giants.

"Nice job," Elaine said.

David shrugged. "I've been practicing." Looking down, he realized the thin sheath of flame still hovered half an inch above his clothing. He didn't know how he did it, exactly, but his mind kept the fire from touching or affecting him. His skin and clothing were untouched even as the fire licked at the concrete beneath him. He extinguished the flames, an act as simple as flipping a switch in his mind, and touched Jessica's shoulder. "Can you still sense them?"

Jessica nodded but kept her eyes forward. "I think they saw Travis. They're heading west after him."

Elaine grabbed David and Jessica by the arm. "Time to move. We have to get Travis first. Get in the car."

The car, parked half a block away, remained undamaged. David sat in the passenger seat. As soon as Jessica had her seatbelt on in the back, Elaine sped off, taking side streets to avoid the disaster area. The sound of sirens came from all directions.

David looked up at the sky. Black smoke covered the sun.

'It's not even noon yet,' he thought. 'How can there be this much craziness in one day?'

Chapter Seventeen

Travis walked cautiously across the parking lot towards a snow-covered path leading into the woods. Ahead, the line of trees stood watch, a great towering wall shutting out civilization.

From somewhere within the woods, a coyote howled.

Travis groaned. "Fantastic. One more thing to watch out for."

He stuck his good hand in his coat pocket; the other rested against his stomach under the coat. Iggy had forgotten to bring him gloves. Traffic noise from the nearby road vanished. The forest swallowed him. The woods maintained the thin layer of snow which had melted elsewhere. A light breeze blew through crisp air, rustling the bare branches and dead underbrush.

Even at midday, the woods felt dark. Travis searched every shadow for a sign of Defksquar.

Something caught his eye. He studied an archway created by two entangled ash trees. The air in the archway shimmered slightly like heat rising off asphalt in summer. The breeze stopped. Nothing in the forest moved.

'Through there,' he thought. It called to him, pulling him off the trail. Frozen knee-high grass cracked beneath his feet as he walked to the archway. Reaching out, he touched the shimmering air. It felt viscous, like a thin layer of warm gelatin. Closing his eyes, he stepped through the barrier. He felt the change immediately.

Suddenly, it was hot and humid. The air buzzed with the whirl of unseen insects. He opened his eyes and saw mighty trees, taller and thicker than anything back home. The smallest soared over 100' tall. Their branches, as thick as a man's torso, were clothed in lush green leaves.

Travis unzipped his jacket and searched for a way forward through the densely packed trees. Then he saw it: a glint of gold.

"There you are." He walked towards the light. Behind him, the coyote howled again. It sounded distant, like a television playing inside a neighboring apartment.

Within minutes, the tree line broke and once again he saw the waterfall.

To his right, the waterfall rose as high as a mountain. The sound of the cascading water was unexpectedly muted, like the call of the coyote. It made him feel like he was between the worlds, neither here nor there.

Above, green birds with yellow wings skittered through the air. An orange sun rose high in the sky. It seemed twice as large as the one back home. Travis looked behind him for a sign of the path that brought him here. There was none. The woods felt intimidating, consuming. He ventured closer to the river.

Defksquar sat at the edge of the river. He stood as Travis approached, a relieved smile on his lips.

"Welcome back." Defksquar twisted the gold ring on his finger.

"Where is this place?"

Defksquar looked back over his shoulder at the waterfalls. "It's called Castle Falls. I draw my power from the planet. I'm strongest in places of natural wonder. This is a sacred place. Spirit is strong here. It's beautiful, isn't it?"

Travis looked above. Dark shapes too big for birds flew in circles above him. "What are those things?"

Defksquar smiled. "Here they're called crystal steeds. I believe you would call them pegasi. They are very shy. This is probably as close as you'll ever get to one."

Travis' eyes went wide as he squinted at the shapes above him. "You're kidding me. Those are freakin' flying horses? They're real?"

Defksquar shrugged. "Occasionally creatures native to my world cross over to yours."

"Like bigfoot? Is he real, too?"

Defksquar closed his eyes. "Ah. I see in your mind's eye what you mean. Those are not creatures of my world. If they exist, they live only on your world."

"What were those things that came after me? Were they from here or my world?"

"A simple question with a very complex answer. Once they lived on Earth. Now they exist somewhere different, a place between the worlds. They are smart and very dangerous. Until today, I believed I had outmaneuvered them, tricked the Orpheans into thinking I was their ally. Their actions today reveal they know my real plan. We have much to discuss but first things first. I promised you I would see to your wounds. Sit with me."

Defksquar sat cross-legged on the ground and motioned for Travis to follow his lead. Once Travis was seated, Defksquar touched the center of Travis' forehead. "Close your eyes and focus on this spot. I will draw the energy of the planet up into your body. Your wounds are not severe. Broken arm, bruised ribs. It will take only a moment to mend you."

"You can do that? Are you some sort of healer?"

Defksquar's shoulder sagged. "A healer? Not as often as I would like to be. When I became a geognost, I took an oath – preserve the biosphere and her children. We believe every life is interconnected. To heal one is to bring balance back to the planet. We only cause harm when it serves a greater good. Even the smallest act may have larger consequences. No being is trivial. Disposable. But I've been at war for so many years, sometimes I forget that."

"If you believe that, why did you torture me and my cousin?"

Defksquar touched his ring. "Like I said, greater good."

Travis could not turn away from the gold ring. Suddenly, his question did not seem important. He closed his eyes and focused on the spot Defksquar had touched.

For a moment, nothing happened.

Then.

"Whoa." His eyes flashed open. Instead of the river and the waterfall, all he saw around him was patterns of colored light. Green energy shot up from the ground through his tailbone and out through the top of his head. It cascaded above him like the branches of a tree. Every part of his body sang. The pain of his injuries faded. Time stopped. He felt suspended in a moment of eternal bliss.

Eventually, the patterns of light faded, as did the feeling of peace. He blinked several times, forcing his eyes to adjust to normal vision again.

"That was incredible," he said. "What did you do to me?"

Defksquar wiped sweat from his brow. "I borrowed energy from the planet to heal you. Now I need something from you. The fate of both our worlds is in your hands."

"Listen, I don't know what you're trying to sell me but I'm…"

"Hush." Defksquar smiled. The gold band glistened and Travis' concerns melted away.

"You are the perfect candidate," Defksquar said. "For my plan to work, I need a pure candidate, unfettered by religious or political views. Your mind is open, a trait more rare than you can imagine. You've lived your life in the shadow of a foramen connecting our two worlds. Genetically, you are untainted, the programming in your cells unpolluted by other influences. I spent many years searching for you. You are the only one who can do this."

"What do you want me to do?"

Defksquar clasped his hands together, hiding the ring. "First, I owe you an explanation. I'll be as brief as possible. Several weeks ago, I lead a party into the ruined city of Te Vark. We sought a collection of advanced machinery called the Miscellany. There was only one item I cared about. The Verdenstab. When we left Te Vark there were 30 of us. We set out for Stone Haven where our ship awaited...but we were ambushed. Seven of us escaped the attack. We hijacked a Nizarian aircraft, a Pharocai, and flew back towards Norshire. We were followed. Shot down by wypera riders."

Travis shook his head, his mind clouded as if in a dream. "I only understood about half of that. Who are the Nizarians? What's a Pharocai? And do I want to know what a wypera is?"

"Large blue and white scaly creatures, easy to mount. They fly and breathe a sort of flammable acid."

"Do you mean a dragon?" Travis asked.

Defksquar closed his eyes. "I see the image in your mind. It is similar to a wypera. But that's not important. Perhaps the details of the story are not important either. I am a stranger to you and no matter what the loss to me or my comrades, we are only unknowns. I will focus on the important matter. The Verdenstab."

"What's a Verdenstab?"

Defksquar waved his hands and an image appeared in the air between him and Travis: a golden rod, three feet long, covered with diamonds, rubies, sapphires and emeralds.

"Whoa!" Travis fell backwards. "Is that some sort of hologram? Did you do that? What is that thing? It kind of looks like a fancy spark plug."

"It is not so dissimilar to this thing you speak of. It carries a current, not of electricity but purified willpower. It allows the person who activates it to alter the reality field of a planet."

"You realize what you're saying makes absolutely no sense to me, right?"

Defksquar waved his hands and the image disappeared. "For now, listen. In time it will make sense. Like I said, though we sought the Miscellany, all I cared about was the Verdenstab. The other items were created by a man named Orpthus. He was a fieldbender, a person able to alter the laws of reality through will. I had no knowledge of the importance of the Miscellany. Then I read Orpthus' journal. I learned the truth. The Miscellany was far more than a collection of random items. It has a purpose."

Defksquar looked off into the distance. "There is a creature, a thing that was once a man. His name, for you, would translate to Lord Dispayre. He's been locked away for centuries. But something has weakened the walls of his prison. Every day I wait is one day closer to his return. I can't risk leaving items this powerful on my planet. That's where you come in."

"When's the part coming where things will make sense?" Travis scratched his head. He had listened to the story, his body still numb. It all seemed so fantastic, and the nervous twitch in Defksquar's left eye did little to add to his credibility.

Defksquar lowered his head and smiled. "Forgive me. This has consumed my life for several years now. I forget myself sometimes. The simple story is this. Years ago I learned of a device so powerful it could reshape the face of the planet. It could create mountain ranges or oceans with a thought. Create new life forms or extinguish an entire species in the blink of an eye. I knew it was too powerful to let fall into the wrong hands."

"You could have used it yourself."

"Unfortunately, no I couldn't. I'm not pure enough."

The light faded in Defksquar's eyes. "As I said, I didn't want it falling into the wrong hands. I know myself too well to trust I would use that power wisely. I needed to get if off my world and somewhere safe. I chose your world. I chose you."

"My planet has connections to eight other worlds, planets I can travel to the same way you traveled here, through weak spots in the reality field. I tested each one. Yours is the best fit. Your world is weak."

"Hey!"

"I do not mean it as an insult. There are few people of power on Earth, people able to alter the reality field. I believe you call them wizards or sorcerers. Activating the Verdenstab there will cause the least amount of damage."

"What do you mean, 'damage'?"

Defksquar looked at his gold ring. For a moment he seemed to weigh a decision. Then he shook his head and continued. "Change cannot come without consequence. But the change I offer will be worth the price. Once activated, the Verdenstab will transubstantiate your world, recreating it into an ideal paradise. Earth will become a place of wonders based upon the blueprints of the Beherskers. Your world will be freed from ignorance and apathy, a happier, healthier place cured of pollution and disease. I've seen the turmoil on your world. Natural disasters increase every year."

Travis frowned. "You're saying this device will fix global warming?"

Defksquar nodded. "Among other things. By taking this device to Earth and activating it, you will ensure it can never be brought back here. It will be forever beyond the reach of the dangerous men here who want it. And you will bring magic to your world."

Travis leaned forward. "What do you mean 'magic'?"

"You've seen the things I can do." Defksquar fingered the gold ring on his hand. "Imagine if the healers on your planet could do the things I could. How many lives could be saved?"

Defksquar spoke in a measured tone, his lips barely moving. But the force coming from behind his squinting eyes convinced Travis he simply had to comply with his demands. Something about his voice made it impossible to refuse him.

For better or worse, Travis decided then and there to follow Defksquar's advice.

Travis sighed and nodded. "How do I activate the Verdenstab?"

Defksquar sighed, relaxing muscles Travis had not seen him tense. "Follow me."

Both men stood. Travis followed Defksquar to a tree near the base of the waterfall. Defksquar reached into the shadows, retrieving a medium-sized leather backpack. Paralyzed, Travis let Defksquar lift the backpack onto his shoulder.

When it was secured, Defksquar smiled. "The Miscellany is inside the pack. It may not look like much, but I assure you its worth is beyond measure. The process for activation is complex. It would take too long to vocalize all the information, so I will plant the instructions to assemble it in your mind. I'll also give you knowledge of the other items. This way, you can retrieve information on them when needed."

With that, Defksquar fell silent for a moment. He closed his eyes, clasped his hands together as if in prayer and then squatted close to the ground. Travis felt nothing at first, then a subtle intuitive knowledge that something was seeping into his mind. He was being enchanted.

"There." Defksquar opened his eyes. "The knowledge is within you now. I will tell you one part because it is crucial. Within the Miscellany, you will find five objects. They are actually small gears but you can wear them like a ring. When you activate the Verdenstab, you must be wearing one of them on your body. If not, the release of the metamorphic powers could destroy you."

Travis paled. "As in kill?"

"As in disintegrate your flesh over the entire biosphere. Don't worry. As long as you do exactly what I told you to do you'll be fine. And both our worlds will prosper." Defksquar turned quickly at a sound coming from the woods. "Damn. They've found me. You have to go. Now. Head back into the woods the way you came. I fear we will not meet again, Travis Froese. It's been a pleasure knowing you. The people on your world will speak of you for all of history."

"Why would they do that?"

Defksquar squeezed Travis' shoulder. "Because you are the man who will save the world." He turned sharply and ran into the woods.

Travis stood alone at Castle Falls, still paralyzed.

Then he heard Defksquar's voice ring out from somewhere in the woods.

"Go quickly. The way back will remain open for only a short time. I can't risk them following you back."

Travis felt his whole body turn, controlled by some outside force. His legs carried him into the woods at breakneck speed. The trail he followed was impossible for his eyes to track. There were no obvious landmarks, only obscurity. He could not tell the moment of transition when he stepped through the outer edge of one world and into the beginning of the next. He only knew that he had returned bearing gifts.

Chapter Eighteen

Wisdom stared down at the scene before them, his mind racing. They stood atop a plateau. A carved stone railing bordered the edge, giving the area feel like a tourist outlook. Below was a valley, as wide and deep as the Grand Canyon. Within the valley was the largest city they'd seen in the Axeinus.

"Unbelievable." To Wisdom's right, Josh crossed his arms and studied the city. "It's so…"

Wisdom nodded. "I know. Beautiful."

"How can monsters create something so beautiful?" Garnet asked.

Skyscrapers, 30 stories tall, dotted the city below. A stone wall dotted with elegant towers circled the city center. Outside the wall, single-family dwellings sprawled out in all directions. Dozens of elaborately carved bridges led from the surrounding cliff walls to the streets below. Large sections of the cavern floor were filled with a black liquid. It moved like water but smelled like wet earth. Small sailboats and gondolas were docked at a nearby marina. They bobbed slightly. They were the only things that moved.

Wisdom shook his head. "There's no relationship between beauty and evil. Some of the most dangerous things I know are beautiful. But this is something I never expected to see again. This city is modeled after Poseidus."

Garnet leaned over the railing. "What's Poseidus?"

Wisdom leaned over the railing. "Dust at the bottom of the ocean, now. Once, it was the capital city of Atlantis. The center island looked much like this but the buildings were made of different materials. Everything here is made out of the same black stone." Wisdom touched the rock wall beside him. "They must have made this valley. Carved it out of rock. When the Orpheans were imprisoned here, they had no tools. It was meant to be a prison. Somehow, they created an entire world."

"It looks empty," Todd said. "Where is everyone?"

Wisdom bit his lip but said nothing.

"Oh," Garnet said. "They must be at the exit, wherever they plan on leaving the Axeinus. I don't understand. This place is not the dark hell I expected. Why would they want to leave?"

Josh looked skyward. "Could you live here? There's no sun. All the light is artificial, fluorescent. I'd go crazy living here."

"That's what I'm afraid of." Wisdom stepped back from the edge and put his hands in his pockets. "Just how crazy are the Orpheans? I expected to find hundreds of them here. The evidence suggests it's closer to millions. They have powers and abilities similar to yours but they don't have your humanity. For so long, they've been locked away. Now they finally have a chance to return to Earth. If they escape, it will be a disaster."

"For humans?"

Wisdom shook his head. "For everyone. Humans still outnumber them. And you have weapons of your own. How long before the first nuclear bombs fly?"

Josh's mouth fell open. "Surely it won't come to that."

Wisdom grinned. "Of course it will. And don't call me Shirley."

Todd laughed weakly. "I think you stole that joke. Is this really what Atlantis looked like?"

Wisdom nodded. "Close. Instead of stone, some buildings were made of glowing pink crystal. Others were metal." He pointed above them. "Imagine a translucent dome over the whole area. It allowed city engineers complete control over the weather inside. Every morning it would rain for a few minutes to clean the streets. The temperature was consistent, the air constantly purified. Oh, I know how it sounds – like something from the Jetsons – but current technology isn't too far away from that. If left alone, you'll probably be there in another hundred years."

Garnet frowned. "What's the Jetsons?"

Todd did a double-take. "Seriously? Cartoon series from the makers of the Flintstones about a family in the future. Flying cars? Video phones? Rosie the Robot? How do you not know the Jetsons?"

Garnet shrugged. "Maybe I was too busy reading while you were watching TV."

"What were they like, Wisdom?" Josh asked. "The Atlanteans. What kind of people were they?"

Wisdom waved the question away. "Silly question. There were two billion Atlanteans. You can't summarize what an entire people are like. Besides, it was a long time ago. I was very young. A child. I don't remember much." He paused for a moment. When he spoke again, his voice was hushed, his eyes distant. "But I do remember Solstice. On the longest night of the year, the entire city went dark and they lowered the force-field. It was the only time of year we could see the stars from the city. People gathered in parks and churches, singing songs. For a few hours everything in the world was magical. My mother, she would…"

Wisdom closed his eyes, pushing the memory away. He took a deep breath and pointed down and to the left. "Look there. That's our way in."

"Are you sure?" Josh asked. "All I see is a broken bridge."

"Exactly," Wisdom said. "That's why we didn't run into any Orpheans in that tunnel. This area wasn't connected to the cities anymore. Maybe they built a new path. Maybe the cities were feuding. Either way, it's the easiest way forward."

Todd exhaled slowly. "You have a strange definition of 'easiest'. That must be a 20-foot gap in the bridge. How are we supposed to cross it without using our powers?"

Wisdom looked down at the abandoned city. "There's no one around. I'll get us across. Too risky to teleport. That sends too much of a power ripple. I'll fly you over."

Todd cleared his throat and looked at the edge.

"Relax, big guy," Josh said. "At least he's not going to throw us."

Todd went pale. "Don't even joke about that."

"Well, then, what are we waiting for?" Garnet walked down the steps towards the broken bridge. "If all those Orpheans are waiting somewhere to get back to Earth, things are much worse than we expected."

'Worse than you can imagine,' Wisdom thought. 'Fighting monsters is bad enough. But we're not fighting monsters anymore. We're fighting a civilization. They don't die as easily.'

Chapter Nineteen

Travis returned to Earth, backpack secured to his shoulder. Its weight helped him realize the trip was real. Nearby, a snowy owl watched him from the forest floor. He blinked.

'Aren't owls nocturnal?' He stared at the owl's large eyes, hypnotized. Then he blinked and the owl was gone. 'Just like the cat this morning. Maybe I am going crazy.'

Leaving the woods, he saw Iggy waiting outside the car.

"Where the hell have you been?" Iggy walked towards Travis, meeting him halfway. "You've been gone for over an hour!"

"Seriously?" Travis looked behind him. "It didn't feel that long."

"What happened to your face?"

Travis touched his face. It felt warm. "Nothing. Why?"

"Dude, you got a red mark on your forehead. Like a sunburn."

Travis looked back into the woods. For some reason he thought about the owl.

"So what's in the backpack?" Iggy asked.

Travis shook his head. "Not here. Let's move. I may have been followed."

"Followed by whom?"

"Did you seriously just say whom?"

"What can I say? I done learned the good English." Iggy pressed the button on his car keys. With a beep, the doors unlocked and they both got in. "Do you seriously think someone's following you? Is it those things from before?"

"Just drive." Travis placed the backpack on the floor between his legs.

Starting the car, Iggy pulled out of the park. They drove back towards the town. Iggy kept his eyes on the rearview mirror.

"So, you met the guy?" Iggy asked. "The one from the hospital?"

Travis nodded. "I think his name is Deafscar or Deadsquar. Something like that. The whole thing was creepy and yet kind of cool. Like traveling to Narnia or something." He wriggled the fingers on his left hand. "He healed my arm. I'll tell you the rest when we get to your place."

"My place? I take it I'm not going into work today."

Travis snorted and shook his head. "You work for your dad. I've seen you call in sick for less. Besides, with what I have, I think we can change the world."

"Have you been drinking the special Kool-Aid?"

Travis smirked. "I'm more inclined to a beer right now. Please tell me you have cold ones in the fridge."

"What am I? A heathen? Of course there's cold beer in the fridge. But you get nothing until I hear what happened to you."

"Fine." Travis leaned back in his seat and watched the city pass by.

Twenty minutes later, they arrived at Iggy's house on Riverside Drive. It backed onto the Detroit River, a three-story glass and steel mansion. Seeing his friend's house always made Travis feel inadequate. Iggy was born into money. That gave him certain opportunities that most people did not have. His father owned one of the major tool and die companies in the city. Iggy was set to inherit the business one day. All Travis was set to inherit from his father was a stack of unpaid credit card bills.

When they got out of the car, Travis looked up and down the street. Normally, Riverside bustled with traffic. Today it was deserted.

Iggy stood beside him. "I know what you're thinking. Maybe we should get inside. I think we'll both feel better behind closed doors."

Police car sirens called out in the distance.

Travis followed Iggy inside, clutching the backpack to his chest like a talisman.

Iggy locked the front door and rearmed the security alarm. "You realize my house is made of glass, right? It's not built to withstand a zombie invasion."

"Who said anything about zombies?"

"Okay. Shadow people. Whatever those things were, they threw cars like paper planes. Shouldn't we get somewhere safe? My family has a cabin up north. There's a tornado shelter there."

Travis took his shoes off. "Because a cabin in the woods is the best place to escape monsters? Get real."

Travis headed towards the living room at the back of the house. Floor to ceiling windows looked out on an amazing view of the Detroit skyline.

Iggy plopped down on the couch. "Are you going to open the bag? I want to see what I'm risking my life for. Empty it out onto the coffee table."

Travis set the backpack on the floor, studying it. It was not decorated with special markings or any arcane writings of warning. Instead, it exuded mediocrity: weather-cracked leather held together by a system of rawhide cord. He reached for the cord, suddenly anxious to peek inside. Noise shattered the silence. He spun around, heart racing.

"Geesh," Iggy said. "Loser. That's just the furnace. You need a beer."

"Maybe after…"

"I wasn't asking." Iggy got up and went to the kitchen. He raised his voice so the sound would carry. "I sure as hell need one and I don't drink alone. You're having a beer."

Alone in the living room, the feeling of being watched returned to Travis. He looked out the window. The backyard was empty. Across the river, the PeopleMover glided along its concrete track. The midday sun glistened off the Renaissance Center. There was no sign of anyone watching him.

Refocusing on the backpack, his fingers deciphered the complex twists and tangles of the rawhide cord. It opened with ease.

Iggy walked back in, a beer in each hand. He handed one to Travis and took a drink from the other.

"Here goes." He gripped the sack from the bottom and, with a graceful twist of his wrist, emptied the contents onto the table. He did not know exactly what he had expected but this was definitely not it.

"Are you sure you got the right bag?" Iggy leaned over the items. "Looks like a bunch of crap from someone's yard sale."

"Hard to believe these things could change the world, eh? This must be the Verdenstab." Travis ran his hands over the largest object on the table: a three-foot-long gilded scepter. When he brushed the dust and grime away, its surface gleamed from end to end. Precious gems seemed to capture the indirect lighting, magnifying it tenfold. The top end was cupped, forming a gently concave opening like the groove where one joint meets another. On further examination, he discovered a smaller indentation at the bottom with three receptacles, forming a triangle, in the middle.

"Well if nothing else, you could pawn it off," Iggy said. He touched the base of the Verdenstab then turned to stare at the backpack. "How the hell did this huge sucker fit in that backpack?"

Travis picked up the backpack and shoved his hand deep inside. He reached for the bottom but felt only cold air. Looking inside the backpack, he saw only darkness. Secretly knowing what he would see, he looked at the outside of the bag. His arm was in the bag up to his shoulder. The bag did not bulge on the bottom. His mouth dropped open and he quickly pulled his hand out.

"Well, that's some Inception-level screwed up crap." Iggy drank the rest of his beer. "I think I need another. You?"

"Hell yes." He stared at his arm to make sure it was fine. "I don't want to be sober for this. Can you bring a knife or something? I want to take this splint off."

He turned to the next largest item from the bag, a massive leather-bound book. He flipped through the yellowed pages, seeing indecipherable text and grotesque ink drawings. Alongside the book was a black dagger with a menacing blade. It seemed to drink in the light around it. There was a gray cloth bag that held what seemed like marbles, a thin gold necklace and five silver rings. The rings were simple, each mounted with identically cut gemstones of different varieties: emerald, sapphire, ruby, onyx, and yellow amber.

"So how do you turn it on?" Iggy came back into the room with two more beers in hand.

Travis started to shake his head, then stopped. "Wait. I think I know." He opened the pouch. Inside were dozens of white glass spheres. He placed one at the concave opening on top. There was a soft suction sound and the scent of dandelions wafted through the room. The marble grew until it was a fist-sized sphere.

"Did that just…?" Iggy slid off the couch and knelt beside the coffee table to get a closer look at the Verdenstab.

"Yep. Grew like magic. I don't think we should pawn this. Wait. Watch this." Travis turned the Verdenstab until he found the largest emerald. He pushed his thumb against it and the rod began to hum. The milky smell of dandelions grew stronger. The air tasted acidic, thick and chalky.

Defksquar's voice spoke in his mind.

The Verdenstab is a fuse, a component in a device used to transform lifeless planets into vibrant geospheres. The fuse itself is not as powerful as the whole device, but you are not starting with a dead world. The Verdenstab transmutes matter and energy along a preset matrix. Without the rest of the machine to feed the preset matrix, it could, conceivably, reshape the world in any way desired by the person who activates it.

Iggy waved a hand in front of Travis' face. "Earth to Travis. Are you in there?"

Travis nodded. "I was listening to the voices in my head."

"We're doomed."

"No, seriously. I could hear Deadsquire-What's-His-Name in my head. It's still talking. It's saying I need to embed the thin end of the Verdenstab in the bones of the Earth. Then press the emerald again. After the energy builds to a certain point, I activate the Verdenstab with a single word. Tower."

"What do you think would happen if you said Gotham City?"

"Not helping. Anyway, according to what the voice is telling me, that word will somehow bypass my individual biases and re-sculpt Earth along the matrix of the planet's Collective Unconsciousness."

"Since when do you know big words?"

Iggy touched the white sphere at the top of the Verdenstab. He jerked his hands back quickly. The surfaced sparked at his touch.

"Careful," Travis said. "It's not a toy." He picked up the five silver rings. "Now he's telling me to wear one of these when I activate it. Somehow it's going to absorb most of the energy released so I'm not evaporated in the process."

Iggy grabbed one of the rings, the emerald and tried it on several of his fingers. "Weird. It fits each finger perfectly."

Travis shrugged and tried on the amber ring. "Yeah. This one does, too. Maybe it's part of their magic. He slipped the ring off and motioned for Iggy to give his back, which he did, reluctantly.

"Bones of the Earth?" Iggy asked. "What does that mean? Just putting it out there, I'm not doing a cemetery."

"I'm not sure." Travis waited for Defksquar's voice to come again.

If you have any questions about the directions I have given you, put on the gold necklace. It is a simple charm of bio-gnostic magic, mostly psychometric in nature. It allows the mind to see beyond the surface structure of languages to understand the deeper structures of meaning. Use its power to read the Grimoire of Orpthus. All your answers will be found there. Put the necklace on, Travis. Do it now.

Travis felt his hands working of their own accord. He slipped the gold chain over his head. There was another sucking sound and the chain constricted slightly around his neck.

Iggy yelped.

"It's okay." Travis touched the chain, pulling it slightly away from his throat. "I can still breathe. Apparently this thing will let me read other languages." He flipped open the leather book and smiled. "Well, what do you know? I can read this now."

Iggy leaned over the book. "Really? What does it say?"

"Give me a minute. I'm scanning here. This thing is like a thousand pages long." He picked up the book and sat next to Iggy on the couch. Flipping through the pages, he saw snippets of ancient history dramas from an alien world. He studied sketches and diagrams where before there had only been blank spaces. He was so enraptured in the ability to understand the foreign language that for a moment he forgot what he was looking for. He came across a section entitled The Miscellany. He settled down to read.

Chapter Twenty

15th of Fjorda, 400 A.S.

I had a thought today. A glimmer of hope. My wounds still tie me to this dank study. Elmontrazar has arranged for a new nurse. Seems the last one found me impossible to work with. As the nurse nattered at me, I realized her accent was familiar. Her intonations were similar to Chark'l sec. He hasn't crossed my mind in years. I threw away my memories of him like tainted fruit. After all, that's what he is now. Durgen saw to that. How sad is it for a man to cease being a man to become only a weapon? Ah, but his memory sprouted a conceit. A hypothesis. Perhaps there was a reason for my dear friend's sacrifice after all. We shall see.

As I studied the Verdenstab, the thought grew clearer. How many years had it sat there waiting, waiting, waiting, always waiting for me to find it? It has a greater destiny than languishing in a rubbish pile in a distant, ruined city. It, like all things, had a purpose. What if that purpose was to end the war?

Of course I do not need to say which war. On Maghe Sire there has only been one war since before the history books were written. The war between the Three Great Castles. What if this artifact designed to transform a planet could instead ʧʑtɛdʒdʒ ʧʑtɛdʒdʒ ʧʑtɛdʒdʒ ʧʑtɛdʒdʒ ʧʑtɛdʒdʒ ʧʑtɛdʒdʒ.

***

Travis tore his eyes away, grunting in pain.

"What's wrong?" Iggy asked.

Travis rubbed his eyes. "It's like the words were on fire in my head. I can't read that section for some reason."

"Did you learn anything?"

"Nothing really useful. I'm going to give it another try. Hold on." Rubbing his eyes, he scanned down the page until he found a section he could read again.

***

With that in mind, I store the Verdenstab with the rest of the Miscellany. Once the Verdenstab is activated, the background energy should re-energize the other items as well. Most important of the baubles are five ring-like fuses. I recreated them based on the ones currently powering Castle Grygar. Each harnesses a different element. But once activated, they will do more than power one of the Great Castles. They will change the world.

***

"I think this guy is kind of crazy." Travis looked up from the book.

"What makes you say that?"

Travis shrugged. "He sounds a bit like a supervillain. I keep expecting him to do an evil laugh or something. Also it says there are about a hundred items in the Miscellany but there's nowhere close to that many in the bag. Here. Listen to this part." Taking a drink, Travis read the next section aloud.

"The blood ring echoes the abilities of the Valgt'til, masters of Nevenbran. It manipulates probability fields. The one at Castle Grygar stabilizes a chaos drive. Once my master plan…"

Iggy laughed. "It actually says master plan?"

"See? I told you." Travis continued reading. "Once my master plan is completed, the recipient will have control over probability fields. They will gain the ability to turn the seemingly impossible into the possible."

"Sounds like we should take it to the casino."

"Seriously?"

"You're right," Iggy said. "Thinking too small. We should hit Vegas." Smiling, he finished his beer and went to the kitchen. When he left, Travis continued reading silently.

***

Each ring mirrors one of the ancient orders that manipulate the reality field. I doubt this is a coincidence. The blood red ring is connected to the power of the Nevenbran. The water ring is connected to the Illuminati (or the Wheelers, as some call them). In Castle Grygar the fuse powers a flux field that safely contains the energy exchange of the other fuses. If successful, my plan will see the recipient covered in a shield of energy, making him invincible.

The third charter, geognosts, focus on the same energy as the tree ring: the ability to manipulate life force. The geognosts use their abilities to encourage plants to grow and manipulate the magnetic subweb of the geospheres. I will change the fuse. The recipient will be connected to the energy field of the planet, becoming, in effect, an avatar of nature.

The fuse I've grown to call the ring of healing bears similarities to the monastic zealots, the elmire ahk. They focus on spiritual enlightenment, the healing of mind, body, and soul. My plan will give the recipient complete control over his own mind, body and soul. His body will be in a state of continuous homeostasis.

***

Travis stopped. "Hey, Iggy, do you have any idea what homeostasis means?"

Iggy sat another beer down in front of Travis. "You realize you totally set yourself up for a gay joke, right?"

"Grow up." Travis rubbed the back of his neck. "We should probably slow down on the beers, too. I'd like to be at least semi-conscious in case I'm running for my life again."

"Speak for yourself." Iggy glanced out into the darkness. "If I'm being chased by monsters, I'd rather be completely hammered. So have you come up with a plan yet?"

Travis shook his head. "Not yet. But I'm almost done this section. Give me a minute."

***

The last fuse is the ring of discord. Just as fieldbenders tear apart and reconstruct the reality field, the fuse at Castle Grygar breaks down molecular bonds to release energy. We fieldbenders are the purest charter, having rid ourselves of the extant flaws in the others. The ring of discord will allow the recipient to disrupt energy fields and dissolve matter.

Also amongst the Miscellany are other items which may…

ʧʓtɛʤʒ ʧʓtɛʤʒ ʧʓtɛʤʒ ʧʓtɛʤʒ ʧʓtɛʤʒ ʧʓtɛʤʒ

***

Once again the writing became illegible for a few lines, covering up what Orpthus was trying to say. Travis skipped down a little further and, once again, the words became legible.

***

The Verdenstab must be partially submerged in the planet to function properly, preferably deep in the bones of the earth, underground in bedrock. To seat the Verdenstab, I'm including the Crescent Dagger. It still retains an element of Balshebar's powers over shadows and the Void. Aside from acting as a portal to her shadow realm, the blade can also cut through any known substance.

Theoretically, once activated, the Verdenstab unlocks the godlike power the Beherskers buried in our genetic code. And that is the danger. Are we meant for that kind of power? Are we ready? The Verdenstab will alter our geosphere to match the collective unconsciousness, altering every inch of the planet to match people's belief structures. Anything we believe to exist, will exist.

The Verdenstab seems to work on the principle that all reality is Maya, an illusion. What we think is physical is simply projections based on the collective perceptions of sentient beings. Since beliefs are not permanent, reality can be altered by changing perception. The Verdenstab gives one the ability to alter the reality field of a planet on a global level. It is frightening to the think of the power the entire machine would possess as it likely contained several thousand Verdenstabs.

***

Travis shut the book. He stared at the closed cover, absorbing the new information.

"So," Iggy said. "What's the plan?"

"I can't do this," Travis said. "If I turn this thing on, the entire world will change. Who the hell am I to make that kind of decision for the entire planet?"

Iggy shrugged. "Who would you trust? A politician? Oprah?"

Travis scoffed and, setting the book down, walked to the windows. "I know our world's in trouble. Global warming, political unrest, war, famine. All that crap. Maybe this thing will make it better. Maybe Defksquar's right and I really could change the world. Save it. But…I need some time to think about this. Everything is happening too fast."

The Detroit River flowed peacefully behind Iggy's house. Travis stared across the water at the namesake city. Detroit was a perfect example of what needed to be changed with the world: so much poverty side-by-side with immense wealth. People in authority abused their power, creating a sickness that led to violence and death. Could there be another way?

A sudden chill crept along Travis' neck. His eyes swept the backyard and the dock to which Iggy's small boat was docked. He took a step back from the glass.

"What is it?" Iggy asked.

Travis shook his head. "I can't see anything but…it feels like someone's watching me. I can feel their eyes on me. I'm not sure we're safe here."

Moving to back to the coffee table, he put all the items back inside the backpack. "I'd love to think about this for a few days but something tells me I don't have time. We have to move. Now."

"Move where?" Iggy went to the window. After a moment he shivered and turned back to Travis. "I think you're right. I feel it, too. Someone or something's out there. We need to get the hell out of here before it makes a move."

Travis swung the backpack over his shoulder. "The book said the Verdenstab had to be embedded deep in the ground to be effective. I know the perfect place. Come on. You're driving."

***

In Iggy's backyard, Carla and Sanchez watched from the shadows, still possessing the stolen bodies.

"Almost time," Sanchez said. "Can you smell it? Something powerful. Do we move now?"

"Soon," Carla said. "Ahriman said the boy would lead us to the Activation site. He's close now. One last push and it's all over for the humans."

Chapter Twenty-One

Defksquar ran through the woods for an hour. Even with his geognost training, his legs grew tired. His lungs burned, but he couldn't stop yet. Behind him, something stirred in the woods. A soft sound murmured through the trees. It told him the Umbral Knights were closing in on him.

'Too risky to fly out,' he thought. With a simple alteration to his bio-field, he could float up through the trees. But it was slow movement, cumbersome. 'The wypera would be on me in seconds. Only these thick trees conceal me. But they won't stop Umbral Knights. The only thing that will stop them from chasing me is traveling through another foramen. But I can't do that. Not yet.'

Ahead, a shallow stream ran along the bottom of a ravine. He altered his molecular density and jumped down. He fell through the stream, deep into the riverbed. The process was called Earth Melding, a specialty of the geognosts. It allowed him to "swim" through earth. He stopped ten feet below the surface, hovering.

'That should throw them off. The rock and water will interfere with their tracking.'

He also knew they would feel him as soon as he resurfaced. Which was why he had to move quickly.

'If I was smart, I'd head towards Karaj Robat. But I have to find out how much the Quadruplex knows of our plans. And that requires a little spying.'

Unencumbered by the rules of physics and inertia, he arrived back at Castle Falls in a few minutes. Rising from the earth was too risky. Instead, he sent his mind up through the earth. Rocks and dirt became his eyes. He saw what they saw.

He expected to find the wypera party who had tracked them since the Te Vark. Instead, he found an army.

'Damn. So many. There must be thousands. I need to get a better look. The Umbral Knights will home in on my location as soon as I surface. I'll only have a few minutes before they can get back here.'

Relaxing his concentration, he slid back up through the earth and rematerialized behind the waterfall.

'Let's see what we're dealing with.' He found a spot where he could peek past the rush of water. From his vantage point, he saw an endless sea of four-foot tall reptilians wearing leather armor. These were members of the Uhyre tribe, a barbaric race allied with the Quadumvirate. Defksquar saw at least 40 taller creatures with pale mauve skin, the Trofast. Their black metal armor gleamed in the sunlight.

One Trofast, larger than the rest, emerged from the crowd wearing bone-white armor.

'Piss and death,' Defksquar thought. 'That's Amir Durgen. Head of the Dem Straki. He's one of the Quadumvirate. What is he doing here?'

Amir Durgen raised a hand. The earth before him transformed, rising up to create a spiral staircase. He walked up the steps until his feet were level with everyone else's head. When he spoke, his voice was unnaturally loud, the result of Amir Durgen's distortion of the reality field. Magic. Defksquar heard it clearly over the roar of the waterfall.

"The human has crossed over with the Verdenstab," Amir Durgen said. The soldiers shouted, their anger and frustration clear.

Amir Durgen waited until the army quieted. "I know. We had hoped to stop the Sirians before they involved another world, but all is not lost. We have the human's scent."

The army cheered, their joy filling the woods.

Defksquar felt the blood rush from his face. 'No. They're going to send an Umbral Knight through the foramen. Travis can't fight that. He doesn't have the power. Not yet.'

Amir Durgen lifted his arms above his head. The crowd hushed. "They tried to close the foramen here to stop us from following. They underestimate the power of the Armies of Dispayre." Again the soldiers cheered. This time Amir Durgen did not stop them. When they quieted, he spoke in a strong, level tone. "It pains me to drag this other world, Earth, into our fight but the enemy has left us no choice. For now we send one Umbral Knight. We don't want unnecessary bloodshed. But if the people of Earth resist, if they refuse to give us back what is ours by birthright, we will take their world by force. Who is with me?"

The sound of the committed cheers was deafening. Defksquar backed away from the mouth of the waterfall. 'I have to get past them, get to Earth and warn Travis. If the Umbral Knight...'

He bumped into something behind him. His eyes went wide, his thoughts quieting. Slowly, he looked up and behind him at the glowing blue eyes of an Umbral Knight. He prepared to alter his density again but he wasn't fast enough. The Umbral Knight grabbed him by the throat and drove his head into the floor.

Defksquar closed his eyes. Pain flooded his mind. Then everything went black.

Chapter Twenty-Two

Iggy turned off the ignition and turned to Travis. "This is a really bad idea."

"It's all I've got." Travis opened the door and stood beside the car. He looked past the 'private property' sign at the Windsor Salt mine. "I mean, we could always try traipsing around in the sewers but, aside from the ick factor, they don't really go down that far. The salt mines are massive. They're as close as we're going to get to the bones of the earth around here."

Windsor Salt had two locations in the area. This one, the Ojibway mine, dated back to 1955. As Iggy drove here, Travis checked the Wikipedia page on his stolen smartphone. Apparently, parts of the mine went down 290 meters, or over 950 feet.

Behind them, an SUV pulled onto the road, heading towards them quickly.

"Someone's coming," Iggy said. "What do we do?"

"Relax. We're not breaking any law. At least not yet. We're still on public property. Probably just someone heading to work. You realize this isn't an abandoned salt mine, right?"

The vehicle pulled up directly behind Iggy's car, the tires crackling on the gravel shoulder.

"Crap." Iggy said. "Do we make a run for it?"

Before Travis could respond, the driver's door opened and a pale redheaded man stepped out. He walked, hands in pockets, towards him.

"Can I help you?" Travis said.

"Finally. You're Travis, right? Josh's cousin?" The man spoke with a faint east-coast accent. His eyes moved back and forth between them. "We've been looking for you for hours."

"Who are you?" Travis asked.

***

David felt relief wash over him. They'd found Travis before the Orpheans. He held out his hand.

Travis shook it, reluctantly.

"My name's David, a friend of your cousin. We're here to stop you from doing something stupid."

"We'll do anything stupid we want." The other man walked menacingly towards him, putting himself between David and Travis.

David sighed and pinched the bridge of his nose. "Look, it's been a very long day and it's a very long story. Why don't we both just get back in our cars and...?"

The man leaned forward, his face close to David's. "Give us the short version."

'Ooh, he's scary.' David heard Jessica's voice in his mind.

'Totally,' he sent back to her. 'Can you and Elaine get out here, please? I'd rather not set this guy on fire if I don't have to.'

Behind him, the front and back passenger-side doors opened. Elaine stepped out but stayed beside the car. Jessica walked towards them.

Jessica, smiling, extended her hand to be shaken. "Forgive David. He's not very good with people on account of him being partially brain dead. My name's Jessica. We've come a long way to find you."

The first man took a step back from David and shook Jessica's hand. "I'm Ignatio. We've had a very long day as well. Why are you here?"

"Here's the short story," Jessica said. "We work with Travis' loser cousin, Josh. A few hours ago we learned Travis was being set up by a man named Defksquar, an alien from a planet called Maghe Sihre. You must be a complete idiot because somehow he's convinced you to set off a device here that will screw up the planet. Which, for the record, would be the dumbest thing anyone has done in human history."

David chuckled. 'And I'm the one who's not good with people?"

'I heard that.' Jessica's voice entered his mind. At the same time, she punched him in the arm.

"How can you know that?" Travis placed his backpack on the ground. "I haven't told anyone except Iggy what's happened to me today."

"This alien isn't working alone," David said. "He's some sort of contract worker for a group called the Council of Peacocks. They're a group of sorcerers trying to take over the planet. Think of them like the Illuminati mixed with Death Eaters."

Jessica frowned. "Hmm. You know, I never thought of them that way before. I don't know what's stranger. The fact that you were smart enough to think of that or that you've actually read *Harry Potter*."

David rolled his eyes. "Look, Travis, we know this is a lot to take in. Why don't we all head somewhere to talk this through? Tomorrow, we can sit down with my boss and Josh…"

"Josh is alive?" Travis said. "Where is he? Does he know about what happened to his mom? After what happened to her, we assumed…"

"He's alive," Jessica said, cutting him off. "Well, he was before he jumped into hell a few hours ago. Come to think of it, he's probably dead by now."

David put a hand on Jessica's shoulder and squeezed. Tightly. "What she means is Josh was alive the last time we saw him, which was only a few hours ago. There's much more to what's going on than you know and…"

Behind them, the SUV they had arrived in flew straight up in the air with a loud whoosh. Elaine shouted something incomprehensible. And everyone scattered. A heartbeat later the vehicle slammed back into the ground, roof first.

David crouched at the edge of the road. "What the hell was that?"

Jessica pointed at a nearby field. Two shadowy people, not the size of normal people, walked towards them.

'Damn,' David thought. 'Orpheans.'

"It's them!" Travis said. He reached down to help David to his feet. "The things that tried to get me at the hospital. At first they were shadows. Then they possessed people and took their bodies."

"We've met," Jessica said.

"We have to move!" David shouted.

Elaine ran towards them in a crouch, gun drawn. "You!" She pointed at Ignatio. "Do you know this area?"

Ignatio shook his head. "No. Not really. But there should be some place up ahead he can hide. This is a huge salt mine. They must have offices or something, somewhere we can lock the door behind us."

David nodded. "I don't think a locked door is going to keep those things out. We know people that can help. An organization called Candleworks. If we get to phone maybe we can contact our offices in New York and have them send help. Now, hustle before the Orpheans start throwing other things."

Chapter Twenty-Three

Defksquar opened his eyes. Something was wrong with his vision. Sight through his left eye was blurred, unfocused. His forehead and left ear felt damp. 'Must be bleeding. Once upon a time, when I was stronger, I would barely have felt that blow. Now, I'm lucky it didn't kill me.'

He tried to move his hands, to check his wounds, but found he wasn't able to move. 'Am I paralyzed?'

"Relax," a voice said.

Resisting the urge to panic, Defksquar looked up. At first he didn't see the speaker. He was too focused on the three wypera who rested by the banks of the river. Over 15 feet tall from foot to head, their torsos resembled the thick, muscular bodies of workhorses. Sky-blue scales covered their backs. While it made them very visible on the forest floor, they were virtually invisible in the sky. The wyperas' thick necks ended in finely sculpted heads. Their long, menacing tails lay on the ground. Each wore a black leather harness.

Someone knelt in front of him, close enough that he could focus on the man's face even with his blurred vision. Amir Durgen.

"You know who I am?"

Defksquar nodded. He tried to speak but the words couldn't form in his throat.

"Can't speak?" Amir Durgen smiled. "It's not uncommon after a head injury. But you know this, don't you? You've seen your share of battlefields yourself, haven't you, Gaysun Defksquar? Oh, don't look so surprised. You're nearly as famous as I am. The alien who came to our world with the powers of the gods only to lose it all in the battle that imprisoned our leader. Because of you, at least in part, Lord Dispayre is imprisoned in the Void. Did you really think I wouldn't recognize you?"

Defksquar lowered his eyes.

Amir Durgen grabbed Defksquar's jaw, forcing his eyes back up. "We have much to discuss, you and I. But now is not the time. I heard back from the scout I sent over. Events on Earth are quickly spiraling out of control. I need to take care of them personally. So I'm sending you back to Castle Dispayre. You'll be imprisoned, tortured. Maybe you'll give us information. But honestly, I hope you don't. I want you to hold out as long as possible. I want you to fight it. Survive until I get back."

Defksquar forced his mouth to work. The words sounded foreign, barely intelligible. "You can't go to Earth."

Amir Durgen laughed. "You're hardly in a position to tell me what to do." He stood and clenched his fists. Invisible ropes wrapped around Defksquar's body, lifting him up through the air to the back of one of the wypera. Amir Durgen waved towards a Trofast. "Get him to the questioning chamber. Give this letter to Myan. Tell her I'll be in touch as soon as I get back from Earth."

Defksquar hung his head. 'If this army is on Earth during the Activation, the process will be corrupted. They'll become part of the process, their thoughts influencing how the world is recreated.'

The Trofast fastened Defksquar to the saddle with thin Nizarian ropes. Then he mounted the wypera himself. As the beast rose into the air, Defksquar looked down at the forest. Thousands of Uhyre tribes marched through the foramen into Earth. Then the wypera turned, blocking his line of sight.

'Too late.' Defksquar closed his eyes. 'I can't stop them now. Time to focus on my own safety. Have to make my move before we get too high.'

His injury made it hard to concentrate but eventually he cleared his mind enough to alter his density. Intangible, he slipped through the ropes and right through the wypera. The trees rushed towards him. Pushing the fear aside, he let himself fall.

'Have to time this just right.' When the ground was only a few feet below him, he manipulated the magnetic field of the planet. A cushion of electromagnetic energy pushed up at his body, slowing his descent. Only then did he re-solidify his body.

In the sky above, the wypera howled.

'That's my cue to get out of here. These woods are too dangerous now. Time to head back to Karaj Robat. The others need to know what has happened.'

Chapter Twenty-Four

Travis ran ahead of the others. The shadow people followed, their pace steady, unrushed. He crossed a half-empty parking lot, heading towards the administrative offices of the salt mine. Ahead, several men in jumpsuits stood in a circle, smoking. Each stared at Travis.

"Whoa, there." An older man with gray hair and a beer gut held up a hand. "Where's the fire, son? You shouldn't be here."

Travis stopped a few feet in front of the group. "Not a fire. Call the police. Then get to safety."

"Why?" A second man, a thin dark-haired Italian, dropped his cigarette on the ground and extinguished it with his heel. "Someone chasing you?"

"Yes." The woman with the gun, Elaine, stopped beside Josh. The men flinched when they saw she was armed but seemed afraid to move. "Now wake the hell up and show us the most secure location."

From the road came an explosive boom. Travis spun and watched fire shoot up high in the air. The sound provoked the men to action.

"Jesus," the beer-belly man said. "Follow me. Hank, call security." Beer-belly man moved at a quick saunter that could not truly be called a run. He opened a glass door into the administrative office, holding it open for everyone. Once they were all inside, he locked the door.

Iggy stared at the door and shook his head. "This is the most secure location? We're doomed."

"He's right," Elaine said. "We can't stay here. This position is not defendable."

"Hold your horses," the beer-belly man said. "We'll get you some place safe. Hank, call security."

Travis shifted the backpack to his other shoulder. 'Well this went to hell quickly,' he thought.

The thin Italian man picked up the phone by reception and held it to his ear. A moment later he set it down. "Phone's dead."

"Don't you have a cellphone?" Elaine asked.

Hank shook his head. "It's in my locker. Salt in the air around here's not good for electronics."

"I've got one," Travis said. He pulled the stolen phone out of his pants pocket and frowned. "Crap, it's dead, too. I could have sworn it was fully charged."

"It probably was." Jessica held her fingers against the glass and looked outside. "These creatures have a way of feeding on energy. That's probably why they attacked the cars. Giant batteries. They'll need that power to stay in our world a little longer. The more they feed, the longer they can stay."

"Could we just wait them out?" Travis stood beside her, eyes darting around for a sign of their pursuers. There saw no sign of them anywhere.

"I don't think they'll give us the opportunity," David said. "We need to get somewhere more secure."

Travis turned to the beer-belly man. "Can you take us into the mines?"

The man shook his head. "You're not really dressed for it, kid. Besides, it's a bit of a hike from here. Even if you run, you're looking at ten minutes of being out there, completely exposed. Just wait for security to get here."

Outside, another car exploded.

"We don't have time," Travis said. He turned to face David. "You had a name for these things. What do you know about them? Do they have a weakness?"

David shook his head. "I don't know much. I'm pretty new to all this, too. Elaine, do you know anything?"

Elaine shook her head. "We know they don't like light. The only way they can exist out here is inside their host bodies. If we kill the hosts, we can send them back. They should be trapped in the Axeinus. Someone must have helped them escape."

Travis turned to Iggy. "Sorry about dragging you into this, bro. How you holdin' up?"

Eyes wide, Iggy shook his head quickly. "Kind of buggin' out here. Good thing I'm not completely sober or I might start to panic. What are we going to do?"

A truck pulled up to the front door. A security guard stepped out and waved at them.

"It's Virgil," beer-belly man said. "He must have heard the explosions. Let him in."

One of the shadow people rose up from a pool of shadow beneath the truck. It quickly grew to monstrous size. Before anyone could open the door, the creature grabbed Virgil. It smashed him into the concrete and then threw him up into the night.

Several men squealed. Travis was one of them.

"We have to get out of here." Travis turned to the salt mine employees. "You should stay here. They're not after you. It's me they want. I'm heading into the salt mine. I need to get rid of this thing."

David grabbed Travis' forearm. "We're not going to let you do that, Travis. If you set that thing off…"

Travis pulled his hand away. "What? What's going to happen if I set it off? You don't know anything. This thing has the power to stop global warming, to put our planet back the way it's supposed to be. The only thing trying to stop it from happening is a bunch of creepy monsters. Doesn't that tell you something?"

Jessica bit her thumbnail. "I don't think it's that simple. It can't be, can it? The Council of Peacocks wanted this to happen. It's been their plan all along."

"I'm right, aren't I?" Travis shook his head, laughing. "You idiots come here and get all in my face an you have no idea what this thing will do."

"Neither do you, Travis," Elaine said. "All you know is what the alien told you. How do you know he was telling the truth?"

A flash of gold light pinged in Travis' head. "I just do. I trust him. Inside this backpack is something immensely powerful. In the wrong hands, it could destroy the world. We have an opportunity to do something amazing, something that could save thousands of lives. Millions. But if those things out there get it, imagine what they could do with this sort of power? You say there's a group of sorcerers out there that want this. Well, they don't have it. I do."

David and Elaine stared at each other, exchanging a long, complex look. In the end, Elaine turned away.

Jessica cleared her throat. "I'm not saying I agree with Josh's dumb cousin but we can't stay here. Underground may be safer. At least there will be no cars for them to throw around."

"But how are we going to get there?" Iggy moved to stand beside Travis.

"You don't have to come," Travis said. "It's not safe."

"No kidding," Iggy said. "Forget owing me a beer. When this is over you owe me a trip to Vegas. But I'm not going to let you run off with a bunch of strangers. I've got your back."

Travis smiled and hugged his friend with one arm. "Thanks. I'm glad to have you. Now if we're going to sneak past these things, we need some sort of distraction."

"Leave that to us," David said. "We haven't told you the whole story yet. There's more to us than meets the eye."

Iggy laughed. "What are you, Transformers?"

"Not quite," Jessica said. Then she jumped into the air…and hung there. A sheath of purple energy encased her body, crackling like slow moving lightning. Cars in the nearby parking lot swirled in a vortex, as if moved by a tornado.

Travis fell backwards. He would have hit the floor, but Iggy caught him.

"What the hell is she?" Iggy asked.

"Question later," David said. "Get to the back door. We'll catch up with you." He unlocked the door and went outside. Then his hands erupted in flames. He pointed at nearby cars and fire streaked across the parking lot, engulfing car after car.

Travis felt numb, vaguely aware he was going into shock. Elaine grabbed his arm, pushing him and Iggy towards the back of the building.

"Move," she said. "Let's not waste this opportunity."

Chapter Twenty-Five

Josh crept forward, looking over the edge of the cliff into the canyon below. Garnet crouched to his right, Todd on the left. Wisdom had taken off somewhere. They hadn't seen him in 20 minutes. Several feet below their vantage point, thousands of Orpheans worked in tandem. Some loaded boxes onto platforms that floated in midair. Others polished and inspected spear-like weapons, their tips glowing with a blue energy. They were not alone.

"I can't believe how many Edimmu are here," Garnet said.

Josh nodded. It was the first time he'd seen the creatures since the assault on Thessaloniki. It was difficult to make out their features from this distance but Josh would never forget them. On average, they stood seven feet tall: reptilian humanoids with leather wings jutting from their backs. He recalled the raspy ululation of their voices and the constant damp sheen of the scales over their faces and hands. All the Edimmu within sight wore identical black bodysuits.

Todd elbowed Josh and pointed toward the end of the canyon. "Can someone explain to me what the hell that thing is?"

Josh looked where Todd pointed and shivered. Bound to a rock wall was a creature shaped like a man but at least 300' tall. Gigantic metal rings encircled its very-human-looking head at the forehead and chin, pinning it in place. Large metal spears pierced its body in various locations. These were connected to tubes that ran down to assorted machinery below. The being was naked and skinless. Its flesh glistened like a festering wound. Its private areas were concealed behind large pieces of machinery that blinked and twirled with artificial life.

Small tumors protruded from various parts of its body, tumors that moved like dreaming eyes behind closed lids. Occasionally, it twitched revealing that it was still alive. However, Josh had no idea how the creature could survive what the Orpheans were doing to it.

"I've seen that before," Josh said. "Wisdom came to me in a dream. He brought me to the Axeinus and we came here. He told me that thing is Argus Propates, the real one. You're looking at a god. Or at least what's left of him."

"So we believe in gods now?" Garnet shook her head quickly. "I can believe a lot of things but I have a hard time believing all those old Greek myths were real. Are we expecting Zeus to make an appearance? There has to be another explanation."

"I'd be happy to hear it," Josh said. "All I know is what Wisdom told me. We spoke more about it the day after the attack on Thessaloniki. He said the Orpheans were using that creature's blood to power their weapon-making machinery. He believes the Orpheans are transferring some of the creature's power to their weapons."

"Look," Garnet said. "Over there."

She pointed to a section of wall close to where the giant, Argus Propates, was bound. A small dot of color moved close to the head. Wisdom.

"What is he doing?" Todd clenched his fists. "He's going to get caught."

Josh shook his head. "I'm sure he can take care of himself. He's gathering intel. That's good. We'll need it before we make a move."

Garnet exhaled slowly. "Let's just hope he gets what he's looking for before that creature opens its eyes."

***

Wisdom wanted to plug his nose to block out the stench of the creature before him but he needed both hands to hold his position on the rock wall. This close to so many Edimmu and an army of Orpheans, he didn't dare use his magical abilities. He already took a significant risk exposing himself this way. But what he was doing was incredibly important. He needed to find out what the Orpheans were doing.

He stopped three feet from the massive head. He studied the needle that stabbed into the creature's right temple. Closer now, he saw the luminescent blue liquid being pumped out of Argus. From this vantage point he could easily follow the tubes down. Just as he feared, a conveyer belt lined with spears and pole arms was being coated in liquid. Where liquid touched metal, the object began to glow.

'How did they capture you?' Wisdom wished he could communicate with the god but, honestly, any communication would put him and the others at risk.

In his long life, Wisdom had met many fantastical beings. He had lived in the fiery dimension of the djinn for thousands of years. He'd seen elementals, angels, and even a dragon once. But this was his first encounter with an actual god.

'Oh the questions I have for you,' he thought. 'How did they find you? According to legend, Argus Propates slew the mother of monsters herself, Echidna.' He sat as gatekeeper for Hera, a role his 100 eyes made him perfect for. 'Of course, legend also says you were killed by Hermes. And here you are, alive and breathing.' Wisdom stopped and looked Argus over again. 'Well, mostly alive.'

Argus' bravery and wisdom inspired a religion: the Argusites. Religious persecution drove them north from Greece, to the lands of Yezidi. When the persecution ended, they left to form the foundation of the Council of Peacocks.

"Where oh where did they find you?" he whispered. "And, more importantly, how can I stop them from doing what they're doing?"

"You can't."

Wisdom turned so quickly he nearly let go of the wall. Hovering in the air before him were three Edimmu. Their wings flapped lightly. Each pointed a glowing spear directly at Wisdom.

Wisdom called upon the fire inside him. His hands flickered with superheated flame.

"No need to fight," one of the Edimmu said. "Ahriman only wants to talk with you."

"We know who you are, Wisdom," another Edimmu said. "But you're completely outnumbered. What were you thinking coming here alone?"

Wisdom's eyes went wide. He looked back to the vantage point where he'd left the others. There was no sign of them.

With a sigh, Wisdom let go of the wall. He used his abilities to alter the density of his body, becoming as light as air. He hovered in place and put his hands over his head.

"Fine," he said. "I surrender. Take me to your leader."

Chapter Twenty-Six

Travis ran out the back door, following Iggy and Elaine. 'Beer-gut guy said the entrance was up on the left just past these buildings,' he thought. 'Let's just hope we get there before those things back there realize we're making a run for it.'

A car exploded behind them. The shockwave reverberated between the buildings. Others came out of buildings all around them, workers in overalls all pointing back at the explosions.

The three of them ran past the workers. A security guard moved to intercept them. Elaine showed her gun and the guard ducked behind a work truck. No one else tried to stop them as they ran over the salt-encrusted ground.

Iggy stopped short when he saw the entrance to the mine. "That looks flippin' creepy. We're not seriously going in there, are we?"

Elaine grabbed him by the shoulder and pushed him forward. "Be a pansy later. Get the hell in there. We need to find a defendable location."

They ran past the entrance to the mine and started the slow descent over paved roads. This part of the mine looked identical to a tunnel: rough, carved out earth.

Travis looked over his shoulder. "How will the others find us?"

"You saw they have certain abilities," Elaine said. "Jessica is telepathic. Don't worry about them. They'll find us."

"What are you guys?" Iggy held a hand against his ribcage, panting as he moved. "Mutants? Aliens?"

"I'm as human as you are," Elaine said. "They're something else. The Orpheans must have a way to track you, Travis. We don't know how effective the stalling will be. Run faster."

Up ahead, a man filled out paperwork by a parked vehicle. He was a thin, white-haired man with a tie barely showing beneath his overalls.

'He doesn't look panicked at all,' Travis thought. 'Maybe the sound of the explosions didn't come down this far. Let's see if we can use him.'

"We need your help," he said. "How do we get down into the mine?"

Seeing him, the man removed bright orange earplugs. He started to say something. Then his eyes fell on Elaine's gun. He gasped and put his hands up. "Don't hurt me. There's nothing of value here. Only salt. Just let me go and…"

Elaine lowered her gun. "Trust me. You don't want to go out there right now. We're under attack. We need to get to safety. How far do these mines go? Where's the safest place?"

The man shook his head, eyes unfocused. "The mines go on for miles. They stretch out all the way under the river and…Look, what's happening? You said we're under attack. Did you call the police?"

Elaine grabbed the man's arm. "Police are not going to help with what's out there. Just answer the question. We need to hide. Point the way."

The man looked towards the entrance and shook his head. "This is a salt mine, not a bunker. Follow me. I know an area most people won't know to look. There's a section of the mine that's closed off at the bottom of the elevator. You can hide there."

"Perfect," Travis said. "Lead on."

***

A shadowy fist slammed into David's chest, throwing him back against the building behind him. The impact knocked the wind from his lungs.

Jessica screamed his name. Then her body floated through the air, landing beside him.

"I'm fine," he said pushing himself to his feet. "We're losing out here. I think it's time we go after the others."

"Absolutely," Jessica said. "Any idea how we escape the giants? I still can't get a fix on them."

"All I got is run as fast as possible. Do you think you can keep up?"

Jessica hit him in the arm. "I can fly, loser. You try to keep up with me."

"I can fly, too. Sorta."

Despite himself, David smiled. Then he saw something new. "Wait. What's that? Is that another Orphean?"

A creature from out of nightmares stalked towards them. It wore a set of black medieval armor that seemed to drink in the sunlight, swirling in place like liquid rather than a solid. Its hands and face were the only parts of its body not covered by armor. They were the most disturbing. Although it looked like a man, the creature had no skin. Raw flesh covered in still-wet blood stood in its place. Luminous energy poured from the spaces where its ears, nose and mouth should have been. In its hand was a massive sword that looked too big for any man to lift, let along wield.

"That's not them," Jessica said. "Can you feel that? It's something else. Something worse."

"We need to go." David pulled at Jessica.

The creature's eyes landed on them. "Give me the Verdenstab. I know it's nearby. I can smell it." His voice sounded like sandpaper against granite. The air grew cold.

"We have no idea what you're talking about," David said.

"Damn," Jessica said, her voice low and steady. "I think I get it. I think he's from the other world. He's probably after that thing Travis has."

The creature turned to look a Jessica. "Yes. Now, where is it?"

David projected his thoughts into Jessica's mind. 'We're out of time. We have to keep it away from him. We don't want something like that to have access to anything that can change the world.' He looked at his hands, clenched them, and then brought back his flames. They covered his hands in a flickering glove.

"Jessica, are you ready to run?"

Before she could nod, the creature lifted a hand and its eyes glowed brightly. The administrative building erupted in flames. Shards of glass from the front windows flew everywhere. Inside, the men screamed as the fire roared inside. David turned away, ducking. When he opened his eyes, he was shocked to discover he was uninjured. Jessica, arms raised, had erected a telekinetic bubble protecting them from the blast.

"Come on, loser," Jessica said. "Let's get out of here before he blows up something else."

Chapter Twenty-Seven

Josh ducked behind a black boulder as the Edimmu led Wisdom away. Todd and Garnet crouched beside him, both keeping low to avoid detection.

"What are we going to do?" Todd asked. "What are we going to do? Game over, man. Game over."

Josh rolled his eyes. "What is it with you and Bill Pullman? Do you stay up late at night memorizing his lines?"

Todd grunted with disdain. "Paxton. Bill Paxton. Seriously, how do you mix those guys up? One's an American legend. The other was in Independence Day."

Garnet turned her back to the rock and sank to the ground. "If you guys are done with movie trivia, can we focus? We're too exposed here. We need to…"

An Edimmu landed in front of them. It stared down at them with glowing red eyes. Its leathery wings flared behind it.

Todd sprung from his crouch and punched at the Edimmu. It grabbed his wrist with scaly claws and flung Todd behind it. Josh aimed lower, punching the creature's knee at a right angle. There was a popping sound and the Edimmu faltered. Before it could respond, Josh punched again, this time a direct hit to its windpipe, collapsing it. The Edimmu clutched its throat but Josh knew it was already too late.

'Only a matter of time before it suffocates,' he thought. He pushed the Edimmu's shoulder. It fell to the ground, spasming.

Garnet rushed over to Todd, helping him to his feet.

"Good job," Josh said. "You're getting fast."

Todd cradled his left arm. "Not that it helped much. I'm lucky it didn't dislocate my arm." He flexed his fingers. "Nothing my TK can't fix."

"Only we can't use our powers," Garnet said. "Wisdom said the Orpheans would sense it. We need to get out of here before other Edimmus come looking for this one. I think I see a way down to the main level. Follow me."

Garnet walked to a narrow opening in the rock wall. Beyond it, stairs leading downward were carved out of the rock. Josh followed her, rubbing his fist. Striking the Edimmu had broken the skin on his knuckles. He wasn't used to bare fist fighting. Ever since the battle of Thessaloniki, he only fought with his telekinetic armor. It was his strongest ability, a sheath of psionic power that covered his body. The armor was resilient enough to repel bullets and punch through concrete. But it wouldn't do him any good if he couldn't use his powers.

Todd cleared his throat. "Seriously, how are we going to get out of here without Wisdom? Do either of you remember the way back to the Stargate?"

Josh sighed. "It's not a Stargate. And yes, I can find our way back."

"Don't count out Wisdom yet," Garnet said. "You saw what he did. He allowed himself to get captured. He'll come find us as soon as he can. My guess? He figured surrendering was the fastest way to get to the Orphean leadership."

"Hmm." Todd rubbed his arm. "Could be. I hadn't thought of that."

The stairwell ended on the valley floor. Garnet lifted her hand, motioning for everyone to stop. Josh peered over her shoulder. Ahead stood a crowd of 40 Edimmu. They examined a row of glowing weapons.

"Eek." Josh leaned close to Garnet's ear and spoke to her in a whisper. "How are we getting past that?"

Garnet shrugged. "You tell me. Your father trained you to be a ninja. What would he do?"

Josh touched his lips, rubbing them as he thought.

Todd stepped forward. "I have a plan."

Garnet shook her head.

"I'm serious." Todd moved to stand beside them and pointed past the Edimmu at a cart lined with boxes. "I know you said no powers but I'm super good at the delicate stuff. You know this. It's what makes me good at healing and picking locks."

Josh grinned. "And cheating at D&D."

Todd's mouth went slack in fake outrage. "You wound me. Just because I get a few natural 20s…"

"I've never seen you roll under 19."

Todd shrugged. "The gods love me. Anyway, I could give a few boxes a nudge. Start them tumbling over. If I aim well, I could cause quite the distraction."

Josh glanced at the boxes. "Might work. But I've got a better idea." He bit his lower lip. "You probably won't like it."

He told them what he wanted to do.

Garnet punched him in the gut. "Are you insane?"

Josh touched her cheek. "Well, insanity does run in the family. But it will work, won't it?"

Josh turned to Todd. "I know I'm asking a lot. Can you live with this?"

Todd nodded. "After what those things did to Bethany and Amy? I have no problem killing them. Don't worry. Do your part, we'll do ours."

Josh took his hand off Garnet's cheek and stepped away from them. He clenched his fists and accessed his power. It was like flicking a switch. It felt the same as getting ready for a game back in high school. Just before he stepped on the court, he turned off one part of his mind and turned on another.

Telekinetic armor formed over his body, an inch above his skin. Immediately, the Edimmu turned towards him, sensing the energy. As they ran to him, claws high, fangs bared, time seemed to slow. Stop.

Then Josh moved. He leapt forward, smashing his armored fist into the first Edimmu's head. The creature flew back 20 feet, bowling over several others. Another Edimmu attempted to grab Josh by the shoulder but its claws could not penetrate the armor.

Josh spun, backhanding the creature. The blow drove it to the ground. A third Edimmu raised its hands from a distance. Inky black shadow shot from its hands like a bolt of darkness. It struck Josh, throwing him back against a rock wall. The shadow spread, swarming over his armor like ants searching for a crack in his defenses.

After a howl of pain, the swarm disappeared. The Edimmu who shot him spasmed on the ground. Josh glanced in Todd's direction and nodded in appreciation. What Josh had asked Todd was simple: use his refined telekinesis to slip inside the Edimmu's body and cause a brain hemorrhage. Simple and terrifying. Intimate. Todd would be inside their minds, feel their pain and terror as they died.

Two Edimmu approached Josh. They moved slowly, determined. Both held metal spears that crackled with blue energy. Behind them, ten other Edimmu with shadow-encased hands pointed at Josh.

'Focus,' he thought. 'Remember the plan.'

One spear-wielding Edimmu circled around Josh.

'Smart tactic. Trying to get behind me. Obviously can't let that happen."

He dropped his armor and focused his telekinesis elsewhere. He grabbed the Edimmu's spear and sent it flying, hurtling towards the ten Edimmu in the distance. They scrambled to avoid it while the other spear-wielding Edimmu stabbed at Josh. He tried to duck but was too slow. The spear's blade sliced into his shoulder. Josh clenched his jaw to stop from screaming. He focused on the Edimmu's knees, using his telekinesis to force it off balance. It faltered. In that moment, Josh brought up his armor again. Just in time. The Edimmu who had tried to flank him punched the side of the armor. Then it screamed and dropped to the ground, twitching.

Multiple bolts of shadow struck Josh, flinging him back into a cart lined with boxes. His armor absorbed most of the impact but left Josh momentarily disoriented. He clawed himself out of the boxes in time to see a dozen Edimmu take to the sky. Their wings flared behind them as they flew towards him.

'Come on, Garnet,' he thought. 'Any second now!'

Then it happened. In the distance, something exploded. Flames and black smoke rose up high in the air. All the Edimmu turned towards the explosion.

'That's all I need.' Josh turned off his armor and ran. He stopped at the far corner of the valley, the rendezvous point. Todd already waited there, arms crossed tightly.

"Garnet's right," Todd said. "You are insane. You don't get to make the plans anymore."

"You did great." Josh put a hand on Todd's shoulder and squeezed.

Garnet ran towards them. She ran into Josh's arms. They embraced for a moment.

"What did you blow up?" Todd asked.

"No idea." Garnet pulled away from Josh. "Something blue and shiny. It looked important. Didn't expect the explosion to be that big. Now what? The Edimmu are distracted but we still have to find the exit point. No relaxing yet. We have an invasion to stop."

"Or you could just let us go home."

Josh spun at the new voice. Once again, he was confronted by the unexpected. A single Edimmu stood nearby. It appeared much older than any Edimmu he'd seen before. The face was thinner, more slender than the others. Its gray-tinged scales sagged, giving the illusion of wrinkles. Although it wore the same clothes as the other Edimmu, the chest protruded in a way that suggested breasts. But it was the eyes that haunted Josh the most. They seemed...kind.

"Is that a female Edimmu?" Todd stared at the creature, fists clenched.

"Who are you?" Josh asked. The Edimmu smiled, its eyes flickering with emotion. It unnerved Josh because those eyes felt familiar. "Wait. Do I know you?"

The Edimmu nodded. "Yes. Joshua Wilkinson, you knew me once upon a time." The voice, like the expression, was more gentle and compassionate than the others. "But this is not the place to talk. Your distraction will only fool the soldiers for a moment. Hundreds will be here in a few minutes. Come with me and I'll explain everything."

Garnet pulled at Josh's arm. "Do you know her?"

Josh shook his head. "I'm...not sure. Defksquar played with my memories so the Council could use me for their plans. I thought I had all my memories back but suddenly...I don't know."

Todd pushed Josh. "Snap out of it. You can't seriously be thinking about going with this thing."

The Edimmu shrugged. "I'm not strong enough to fight you. Come with me or stay and fight. Decide quickly. Time is running out. Please, Joshua, give me a few moments for old time's sake. I can hide you long enough for us to have a conversation. And I can tell you where your father is. Once you have all the information, you can decide what to do."

Josh frowned. "What do you mean 'all the information'?"

The Edimmu smiled, turned and started to walk away.

"Damn it." Josh closed his eyes in frustration. He turned to Garnet and Josh. "Come on. Let's follow her and see what she has to say."

Chapter Twenty-Eight

"Duck!"

At Jessica's warning, David threw himself to the ground. It was just in time to avoid one of the shadow giant's fists. He rolled himself back to his feet and blindly shot flame in the giant's general direction.

There was a howl of pain followed by a flash of blue light. A wave of concussive force struck David, pushing him off his feet. His head struck concrete. It wasn't hard enough to cause serious injury but he did have the wind knocked out of him. Then Jessica was beside him, pulling on his arms.

"Get up," she said. "We have to go."

David pushed her off and got to his feet. He searched for the giants but they were no longer focused on him. Both fought the hellish creature in armor. It swung its massive sword at one of the shadow giants. The blade sliced through the giant's arm, severing it. The other giant slammed a fist at the monster, smashing it into the ground.

Jessica stomped on his foot.

"Hey!" David yelped.

"Stop gawking and run. Unless you want to be here to face the winner. Let these things fight it out."

David nodded and they both ran away from the battle.

"The others are up ahead," Jessica said. "I can feel them heading down some sort of elevator. Elaine must be trying to find the best defensible place. We need to tell them about this new thing."

"If we *can* defend ourselves." David looked back. The sword-wielding monster raised its weapon. Blue energy shot from the weapon and struck one of the shadow giants in the chest. "Can our luck get any worse?"

***

The salt mine employee opened a locked door. Travis stepped inside as their guide flicked a switch. Cold light illuminated a storeroom lined with empty shelves.

"How far underground are we?" Travis looked around. He saw only one entrance.

"About 920 feet below street level," the man said. "We're not far from the main salt bed. Most don't know there's a storage room here. You're as safe as you're going to be. Stick tight here. I've got to get back to work."

"You're totally going to call the police, aren't you?" Iggy asked.

The man looked at Elaine's gun.

Elaine holstered the gun and raised her hands in surrender. "Fine. Go call the police. Better yet, call the army. At this point it couldn't hurt."

When the man left, Travis took the backpack off his shoulder. He placed it on the ground beside him and stared at it.

"Don't think about it," Elaine said.

Travis shot his eyes up. "I wasn't–"

"Yes, you were." She walked away from him to study the door. "You were thinking of turning that thing on. You still don't get it. Defksquar brainwashed you, Travis. He has some sort of magic ring that plays with your mind. I don't know how he does it. These people with all their powers…they have no concern for regular people. They use us. You can't trust your own mind when you're around them."

"Do you trust the people you came with?" Iggy tilted his head to the side. "David and Jessica? Do you trust them?"

Elaine sighed and rubbed the back of her neck. "I'm not sure how to trust. But can you honestly tell me this alien, Defksquar, is beyond reproach? Don't you think it's at least possible he's been playing you?"

A flash of gold twinkled in Travis' mind. He shook his head. "No. That's not possible. I trust him. I'm going to activate the Verdenstab. If I'm right, we could save the planet. Isn't that worth the risk?"

Before he could react, Elaine was on him. She moved too quickly for Travis to see how she did it. All he knew was that, now, he was on the floor and she crouched above him, gun to his head.

"What if you're wrong?" she asked. "Turn that thing on and you doom the planet. Millions could die. Is it worth the risk?"

Something slammed against the door making them both jump.

"Let us in!"

Elaine put away her gun. "It's not locked, David." She stood up and walked to the door. Travis stayed on the ground for a moment, still shaken.

David and Jessica scrambled into the room.

"The door doesn't lock?" Jessica stared open-mouthed at Elaine. "How are we supposed to make a stand here if the door doesn't even lock?"

"Move." David pushed Jessica aside and extended his hands over the doorframe. The metal heated up, fusing as David welded them inside.

"Are you insane?" Elaine rushed over to him. "That's our only escape. How are we supposed to get out now?"

"I'm more concerned with keeping that thing out," David said. He blew on his hands, which were no longer covered in flames. "We have a bigger problem now. Something else is out there. Something new. Worse than the giants."

Travis listened as David and Jessica quickly told them about the creature in black armor following them.

"We caught a glimpse of it as we entered the elevator," Jessica said. "Which means it killed those giants. It's only a matter of time before it finds us. We have to come up with a new plan or we're done for."

Travis knelt down and opened the backpack. He started taking out the items inside.

David went to Travis and knelt beside him. "You can't use that thing. You just can't."

Travis did not look at David. "You said we needed a plan. I have one. Everyone is after this thing. Once I activate it, once it's turned on, it won't be any good to them anymore. It's the only play we have left."

Jessica stamped her foot and swore under her breath. "Josh's idiot cousin is right. Damn it. It's the only thing we can do."

"But if we do that, the Council of Peacocks wins," Elaine said. "Everything we've done to stop them, everything we've lost was for nothing. Wisdom will not be happy about this."

David exhaled slowly and sat down on the floor. "Well, Wisdom's not here, is he? If he was, he could just teleport us away to safety. We're on our own now. I'm not ready to die yet. Are you?"

Elaine crossed her arms and pursed her lips.

Travis held the five fuses in his hand and stood. "We have one bit of luck. Once I turn this thing on, activate it, it will release vast amounts of energy. Defksquar told me it would kill anyone close to the Verdenstab unless they were in physical contact with one of these. You can wear them like rings. Somehow they adapt to the size of your finger. Don't ask me how. It's like magic."

Jessica's face went pale. "Don't you think that's a little convenient? There are five of us in the room. Why did he give you five rings if you only needed one?"

Iggy knelt beside Travis. "She's right. That does sound a little too convenient."

Elaine clenched her fists. "I told you not to trust Defksquar. He's probably arranged events to make sure we were all here."

"But why?" David rubbed his forehead. "What's in it for him? And how? The only reason we're here is…" David stopped and punched the floor. "Well, fuck me."

"What?" Travis glanced back and forth between David and the others. No one would look him in the eye. "Why are you here? What happened?"

Elaine laughed under her breath and put her hand to her forehead. "Ms. Ryerson. She overheard a few Council members talking. They said you would activate a device that would change the world. It never even crossed my mind that they wanted us to hear that. I can't believe I was so stupid."

"Well. I can," Jessica said. "No offense, but you're nowhere near as smart as you like to pretend you are, Elaine. So what are we going to do now?"

Something slammed against the door. The sound jarred them. David jumped back to his feet.

"We're out of time," Travis said. "However you ended up here, whether by accident or as part of Defksquar's plan, the only thing we can all agree on is this. We're trapped and being chased by things we cannot fight. But there is something we can do to stop them. All you have to do is put on the fuses and let me activate the Verdenstab."

Something pounded against the door again. This time the walls shook.

"Or we let that monster get its hands on it."

David held out his hands towards Travis. "Give me one. Let's do this."

Travis slipped the amber ring over his left ring finger and passed the ruby ring to David. Jessica received the sapphire ring. Iggy and Elaine received the emerald and onyx rings respectively.

Jessica shivered as she placed the fuse around her finger. "This thing feels weird. Like it's nibbling on my finger. I can almost hear it thinking."

"You won't have to wear it for long." Travis grabbed the dagger and stabbed into the ground. The earth rumbled as the ground split apart. "From what I understand, we can take them off as soon as the Verdenstab is activated. Is everyone ready?"

Travis checked to ensure everyone had put on one of the rings.

Elaine turned to David. "For the record, I'm going to blame you for everything."

David reached forward, grabbed Elaine by the neck and kissed her passionately on the lips. For a moment Elaine resisted. Then she surrendered to the passion. She raised her hands and touched David on the cheek.

Jessica made gagging sounds.

David stepped back, smiling. "Now I'm ready."

Travis gripped the Verdenstab tightly in both hands and jammed it into the hole in the ground. It went in easily, sliding into the floor up to its mid-point. A sound filled the room, as soft as a whisper. The orb at the top glowed. A light – pastel blue – illuminated the room.

The five gathered silently around the glowing orb, falling into place with the ease of an often-repeated ritual. All were straight-faced, and despite their fear, strangely at ease. They each closed their eyes on some silent cue.

Travis took a deep breath and said the word.

"Tower."

Chapter Twenty-Nine

Wisdom walked down a stone hallway surrounded by Edimmu. His hands were in front of him, bound by electronic handcuffs.

"These are new," he said to the Edimmu on his left. "The design is old – Atlantean, if I'm not mistaken – but it incorporates new Candleworks technology."

The Edimmu poked him with a glowing spear. "Keep moving."

Wisdom jumped as an electric jolt coursed through his body. "Hey! Watch the suit. It burns easily. So where are you taking me, anyway?"

"Lord Ahriman waits for you in the throne room."

Wisdom smirked. "Seriously? He has a throne room? What is this, *Game of Thrones?* Who actually has a throne room anymore?"

The hallway ended at an immense gothic archway. The Edimmu stopped at the entrance and motioned for Wisdom to continue forward.

He nodded. "I see. I get a private audience. Thanks for the escort. Is it customary to leave a tip?"

Each of the Edimmu stared back at Wisdom, silent.

"Tough crowd." He passed through the archway into a large open area that resembled a cathedral. He walked down an aisle lined with red carpet. Row after row of stone pews lined each side. At the far end of the room sat a massive throne carved from black stone. Ornate pillars rose high above to a ceiling covered in shadows. The shadows were not empty. Dozens of red, glowing eyes looked down at him.

"Do you like what I've done with them?"

The words came from somewhere above him. It sounded like five different people speaking at the same time, each voice a different pitch and tone. They echoed throughout the throne room, making it impossible to pin down the speaker's location. Wisdom inhaled sharply as he realized to whom the glowing eyes belong. He turned in a slow circle, trying to look as nonchalant as possible.

"Nice to see you still have a brain. So rare to find someone who can actually think. After you destroyed the Council's base in Thessaloniki, we moved the rest of the Council off Earth."

"What about Lucius? I've seen him around. Why leave him?"

"Ah. Yes. I suppose this is the point when I'm supposed to reveal my entire plan to you. How boring. Lucius has a purpose like all the other players. I'd much rather talk about the Anomalies. We put each of them through the process of Eyeness. The Council believes the process forces humans to evolve. But we know better, don't we, Wisdom?"

Wisdom walked towards the throne, unsure which part of the shadows to talk to. "Do we? It looks like evolution to me. I assume you believe humans can't evolve."

"Of course not. Robots don't evolve. They are simply recoded. Reprogrammed."

"How many survived the process?"

Something flew above him in the shadows. "Fifteen. Sadly, the mortality rate was higher than expected. Most robots can only survive the first stage of evolution. The half-breeds had some true Atlantean blood in them. That increases their odds of survival."

Wisdom grunted. "They're not robots, you idiot. They're human."

"Same thing."

"And you're not Atlanteans. Not anymore." Wisdom stared at the ground. "Part of me wants to know which ones survived. I found each of them, was involved in their lives. But they're gone now. All of them. Whatever is left, they are not the people I knew before."

"On that point we agree." The voice grew louder, giving Wisdom a better sense of where it came from. He turned to the upper left in time to see a shape descend from the shadows. It was significantly larger than any of the other Orpheans. The speaker was heavily muscled, at least 15' tall and 5' wide at the shoulder. It wore a red sleeveless tunic that hung past its knees over black pants. Its bare arms were covered in flesh as red as newly-poured blood. Large ram-like horns curved upward from its forehead. Bulky bat-like wings fluttered behind the creature. Yellow eyes stared back at Wisdom, glowing in the shadows.

Wisdom's jaw dropped. "Ahriman. What happened to you?"

The creature smiled back at Wisdom, a big toothy grin revealing multiple layers of teeth. "I evolved. Do you like it?"

"You've become a monster."

"That's funny coming from you." Ahriman landed in the aisle a few feet in front of Wisdom and walked towards the throne. "How many people have called you a monster over your long life? Your support of the Tang dynasty during the An-Lushan rebellion? The Muslim conquest of India? The Druidic purge? You are in no position to call me a monster."

From the shadows above came whispers and high-pitched giggles.

Wisdom followed Ahriman to the throne. "Seriously, what happened to you? Is this the Disease?"

Ahriman spat. "This is no Disease, heathen. It is science. Progress. Our forefathers re-mastered our DNA, granting us genetic superiority. We would have won the war but those cowards, the Law of One, broke the world. They sank our homeland, all the while passing judgment on us because we looked different. Nowadays, even humans realize that is racism."

"You turned yourself into a demon."

"Demon is a relative term. My enhancements are the next step in our evolution, a new level of supremacy. I will pass them on to my children. All thanks to one new injection. Can you guess the substance?"

Wisdom looked back over his shoulder. Suddenly the answer was simple. "Damn. You injected yourself with the blood of Argus Propates."

"Correct." Ahriman applauded and cocked his head to one side. "To tell the truth, you were actually our inspiration."

"I know I'm going to regret asking, but how exactly did I inspire you?"

Ahriman leaned forward on the throne, his smile wider than ever. "For thousands of years, my people have been exiled in the Axeinus. Using magic and mirrors, we've watched as humans spread like a plague over our world. Then, we saw you, a son of Atlantis who escaped the flood. Historians record your rise to power, the way you infiltrated political arenas. I became obsessed with you in the Middle Ages. Do you remember Gilles de Rais?"

Wisdom frowned. "The child killer? He tracked me down in the late 1430's. He wanted to be my apprentice, to learn how to control demons. I told him only amateurs dealt with demons."

Ahriman folded his hands in his lap and leaned back. "Perhaps. But we used Gilles de Rais. He proved to be very useful. All he wanted was a long life and endless riches, something you already had. When you refused, he came to us. Gilles filled in the gaps we had in your history. We learned how you achieved your powers. My father realized how mutable our people were and devised a process. If something like you could be created by mixing djinn and Atlantean DNA, what would happen if we were infused with the power of an actual god? Finding one was difficult but we had nothing but time. You are to thank for everything I am today. Your people thank you."

Wisdom clenched his fist. "Let's get one thing straight. The Orpheans are not my people."

Ahriman waved the insult away. "Deny your heritage all you want. You were born Atlantean. So was I. Like it or not, we are family. You have so much power. So many connections. Tell me, why have you never tried to rule the world?"

Wisdom grunted. "Only crazy people want to rule the world. It's hard enough running a few corporations. Besides, if you're at the top of the mountain, everyone else just tries to knock you down. I'm getting bored, Ahriman. Are we going to fight or what?"

Ahriman leaned forward. "Oh, we're not going to fight, Wisdom. There's no point. The war is already over. You just don't know it yet."

Wisdom stuck his hands in his front pockets, frowning. "I'm not admitting defeat just yet. I have agents in Windsor. They'll stop the Activation."

"They've already failed." Ahriman smirked and waved a hand behind him at a floor-to-ceiling mirror. As Wisdom watched, the mirror fogged over with gray mist. The mist slowly faded away, becoming a window into another location. He saw David, Jessica and Elaine in what appeared to be a basement storage room. He could not hear what was being said but the situation was clear based on their actions. David shouted while pointing at a metal door in the background. Elaine yelled at David, apparently trying to talk him out of something. There were two other men in the room. Wisdom recognized one of them as Josh's cousin, Travis.

Wisdom moved closer to the mirror. "What am I looking at?"

"Your agents, as you call them, have barricaded themselves inside the Windsor Salt Mines. You see, Wisdom, I took steps. I've never trusted the alien, Defksquar. It was always possible the enchantment would fail at the last moment. Maybe Travis would realize how dangerous the device was or someone would talk him out of it. They attacked him, backing him into this corner. He sees only one escape now. He's about to take it."

Wisdom's fists unclenched slightly. "He won't turn it on. Elaine will never allow it."

"Really? Even if it means her life?"

"Yes. She's a good soldier."

"Perhaps. Thankfully, we'll never know. Because the situation is even more clear cut now. When Travis brought the device to Earth, he was followed. Outside that door is a creature of darkness, something far worse than one of my agents. They won't let the device fall into its hands."

Wisdom studied Elaine's face, watching the complex series of emotions play out on her face. "She can't. Come on, Elaine."

Ahriman rose from his throne and went to stand beside Wisdom. They watched as Travis unpacked the items and distributed the ring-like fuses.

"This is the point, Wisdom." Ahriman took a deep breath. "Can you feel it? This is the moment the world changes. The best part is Travis truly believes the lie."

Wisdom narrowed his eyes. "Explain."

"Defksquar told his pack mule something that is partially true. Activating the device will save the planet. It will end hunger and poverty."

"Bull."

"Not at all. That part is true. What he doesn't realize is how it will end poverty and hunger. But I won't spoil the surprise. I'll show you as soon as the device is activated."

"Show me how?"

Ahriman spread his hands out, motioning towards the mirror. "Mirrors are magic, a perfect gateway. With a little training, you can use them to see the future or communicate over vast distances. It's actually how we first made contact with Defksquar. More importantly, there are reflective surfaces all over the world. I can connect you to each one." Ahriman turned and went back to his throne. "I've learned something about you over the years. You have too much faith in the robots."

A fire flamed in Wisdom's eyes. "You know, you almost had me. For a moment, I almost believed you were going to win. Then I remembered something. You're a pompous idiot. I know because I spent most of my life being one. You sit in this ridiculous throne room with toy monsters you created from children and you taunt me. If you've really been watching the world for thousands of years, you should know that's a dumb thing to do."

Wisdom extended his hand and threw a spear of flame at Ahriman.

With a flick of his wrist, Ahriman deflected the flame. "I told you, we are not going to fight."

"You can do whatever you want. Me, I'll be fighting."

Before Wisdom could attack again, someone entered the room behind them. Wisdom did not have to turn around to recognize the voice belonged to Richard Wilkinson.

"Master. He didn't come alone. Someone blew up a plasma generator."

"Leave them," Ahriman said. "There's nothing they can do to stop us. Continue with the…"

A wave of energy shot through the room. The effect was nauseating. Wisdom fell to his knees, his head swam with vertigo. As quickly as it came, it passed.

Pushing himself back to his feet, he looked around. Ahriman had been knocked to the ground as well, but he wasn't pushing himself to his feet. Instead, he lay there, back to the throne, laughing.

Wisdom took a step closer to Ahriman. "What was that?"

"That was the device," Ahriman said. "It's just been activated. We won."

Chapter Thirty

The female Edimmu led Josh, Garnet and Todd to an opening in the cavern wall. They walked quickly down a hallway lined with electric lights and a carpeted floor.

"Where are we going?" Josh asked.

The Edimmu raised a finger to her lips, motioning for silence, and continued forward. Moments later they arrived at a wooden door. The Edimmu looked up and down the hallway, unlocked the door, and motioned for them to go inside.

Josh looked around the room. 'Is this a library?' Elegant stone bookshelves were carved into each wall. A long table filled the center of the room with low benches on either side.

The Edimmu closed the door behind them and pulled something from beneath her peacock robes. Josh clenched his fists in preparation only to relax when he saw what the object was: a book.

Garnet looked at the shelves. "Is that what you expect us to believe is in all those boxes. Books?"

The Edimmu smiled. "Solid deduction. Some boxes. Not all. Others have pieces of art – painting, sculptures. The Orpheans have been imprisoned for millennia. A people cannot live that long without developing art. This room was my personal library. Each city had at least one library 50 times larger than this one. The Elders thought it important to take our history with them."

Josh shook his head. "Who are you? And why do you seem so familiar?"

The Edimmu sat on the bench and motioned for the others to sit across from her. Garnet and Josh did. Todd chose to remain standing.

"My name is Ereth Chisti," the Edimmu said. "Call me Ereth. We met several times when you were a child. The Council of Peacocks and that alien, Defksquar, played with your memory so much I'm not surprised you don't remember. When you were younger, before they realized how dangerous you were, Richard Wilkinson often brought you to the Axeinus for training."

Josh wriggled uncomfortably in his seat. "Training for what?"

Ereth rubbed her hand over the front of her robe. "I'm afraid I don't know much. Little people like us are seldom informed of our leaders' activities. I believe you met with combat specialists on ways to enhance your abilities. Richard Wilkinson always said he had big plans for you. At the time, he was very proud of you, much like I am of my children."

"You have children?" Todd spat the question like it was a curse.

Ereth nodded. "Three. Two daughters and a son. They are with their father in our mountain base in South America. I haven't seen them in years."

Garnet leaned forward, placing her forearms on the table. "You have a base in South America? You mean this isn't where all the Edimmu are?"

Ereth's eyes went wide. "Here? No, child. Hardly any Edimmu are inside the Axeinus. Most live in underground cities back on Earth. Although our numbers are nowhere near as great as they once were, we are beginning to thrive again. In large part, that is thanks to our working relationship with the Council of Peacocks. Many have been able to buy freedom for their families."

Garnet frowned and glanced at Josh.

Josh winced. "Are you saying you're slaves to the Orpheans?"

Ereth averted her eyes, staring at the book she'd placed on the table. "That is…not a word the Atlanteans use. To them, we are *caethes*, one who serves." Her shoulders slumped and a weak smile spread over her lips. "But perhaps slave is a better word. We lost our own language long ago. Now, even our thoughts are Atlantean thoughts. I only know your language due to my position as an emissary and the work I've done with the Council of Peacocks."

Garnet tilted her head to the side. "Why aren't you with your children?"

Ereth looked at the door. "My position makes it difficult to leave. I have a degree of influence. I used it to send my family to safety. But if I leave, so does my influence. My husband was a carpenter. Now he sits on the senate. There are tens of thousands of us there, living in underground caves. That is why I implore you to stop fighting this battle. If you let the Atlanteans return to earth, my people have a chance. For the first time in thousands of years we can stop living in the dark, underground. We may finally get the chance to live in the sun again. Our wings were made for flying, not cowering in the dark."

Josh covered his mouth with his hand, completely unsure of what to say.

Ereth opened the book and turned it so it faced Josh.

Josh leaned forward to better focus on the pages. Ereth had opened the book to a two-page spread. On one page was a series of symbols Josh interpreted to be writing. It was definitely not English. He could not understand any of it. A watercolor painting filled the opposite page. It showed an Edimmu, wings raised, speaking to a group of human teenagers beneath an apple tree.

Josh shook his head and looked up at Ereth. "What am I looking at here?"

"You've got to me kidding me," Todd said. "Can't you see what she's trying to do?" Todd came forward and pointed at the picture. "That is supposed to represent a tree in the Garden of Eden, the tree of knowledge. She's trying to convince us that the serpent in the Bible was actually an Edimmu."

Josh scoffed and rolled his eyes. Then he noticed the serious expression on Ereth's face. The smile fell from his lips.

"Wait," Garnet said. "You're serious. You believe it was one of your people that taught humans about good and evil?"

Ereth shrugged. "That is the legend. You have your myths, we have ours. Do you know the etymology of your word, Eden? It comes from an Akkadian word, edinnu, meaning grassland. My people were once called the Edinnu. According to our legends, that is where we lived, on a vast fertile plain. The Edinnu were the first people of this planet. After us came the Neanderthals and the Lemurians."

Garnet shook her head. "What's a Lemurian?"

Ereth sighed and hung her head. "There are very few Lemurians left. Perhaps a few thousand at most. They live in the forests of the world far from human civilization. Legend tells us that beings from the stars came and used magic to evolve certain tribes of Neanderthals into great intelligent beasts. Before the time of Atlantis, they established an advanced civilization in what is now the Pacific Ocean. They stand 12 feet tall, their bodies covered with thick orange and brown fur."

A shiver ran through Josh as another vague memory resonated in his mind. "Oh. Sasquatch. That's what we call them. I think I've met with them before."

Ereth nodded. "Your father worked with the Lemurians when he was a member of Candleworks. It makes sense he would have introduced you to them."

Garnet pulled the book closer and flipped through it. "I saw pictures of one once. Hard to believe there was a society of Bigfoots. Or is it Bigfeet? Never mind. Tell us about these beings from the sky."

"In our history books, the people from the stars were called Beherskers, an ancient name meaning Masters. The Lemurian civilization worked in harmony with the Masters and my people. Then the Atlanteans appeared. We are not sure where they came from. Some say they were engineered by the Masters but the Atlanteans do not admit that. They claim they evolved naturally. The Atlanteans and the Masters did not get along. There was war. The Atlanteans lost, of course. You cannot fight a war against the gods and win. For centuries, the Atlanteans struggled, cold and naked in the wilderness. No one came to their aid for fear of incurring the wrath of the Masters. Once the Masters left, the Edinnu sought out the Atlanteans. We taught them the secrets of agriculture and math. Civilization. We stayed on the outskirts of their civilization, never interfering, only guiding. They came to refer to us as the Watchers, or the Grigori."

"I'm a Christian," Todd said. "And I've spent more than enough time in church to know that Grigori is another name for fallen angel. Josh, don't trust her. She's just admitted her people are demons."

Ereth closed the book. "Some have called us that, yes. But my people did many good things for the Atlanteans. That all changed with the creation of humans. The Atlanteans view you as nothing more than toys. Robots."

"We've heard that story," Garnet said.

"Really?" Ereth smiled. "Surprising. Few humans know it. After Atlantis fell, a flood overtook the world. My people moved underground and, for a time, we were separated from the other races. When we met the Atlanteans again, they had changed. They had unusual abilities. A darkness flowed through them. A disease.

Some could turn their body into pure sentient darkness. Others boasted control over the elements. Whatever had happened to them, it made them brutal. Violent. They imprisoned my people. We've been slaves ever since."

Todd clenched his fist. "Just because Edinnu and Edimmu sound similar, that doesn't mean there's any truth to your story. Josh, snap out of it. We need to get out of here and rescue Wisdom."

"In a minute," Josh said. "If you are slaves, Ereth, why do you want us to help the Orpheans?"

Ereth focused her eyes on Josh and stared, unblinking. "I care little for the Atlanteans, the people you call the Orpheans. My concern is for my people. If we stay, nothing will change. Our only hope of freedom is to return to the world. The only way we can return is if they do."

Josh scratched his chin. His mind whirled with information. He wasn't sure what parts of the story to believe. It seemed impossible but Ereth spoke with sincerity. True or not, she believed it.

"Damn it!" Todd smashed his fists down on the table. "What the hell has gotten into you, Josh? Do you remember what they did to us? What they did to my friends?"

Ereth turned to look at Todd. "Please do not judge my entire people on the actions of a few. We call our soldiers Nagas, a term many humans still recognize and fear. They are cold, ruthless monsters who drink human blood for sport. Those chosen to become Nagas are separated from their parents early in life. Taught to suppress, to focus on their rage. Would you judge all of humanity on the actions of your soldiers?"

Todd's nostrils flared. "Human soldiers don't break into people's homes and steal their children."

Ereth narrowed her eyes. "Either you are truly naïve or you are lying to yourself. Maybe soldiers in your country do not do such things. But do you truly believe all soldiers in all countries act as ethically?"

"Maybe not," Josh said. "But Todd's right. The Edimmu have done some very horrible things. We have reports of reptilians sacrificing babies and drinking human blood. I watched as they kidnapped my best friend when I was younger. They killed him for no reason. How do you explain that?"

"You're speaking of Tommy, of course." Ereth bowed her head. "I warned you once to stay away from Tommy Delonki. He was not what you thought he was."

Josh's eyes went wide. "You! I remember now. You were one of the Edimmu I caught sneaking into his room."

Ereth touched her face. "Yes. You slapped me pretty hard."

"What do you mean, he wasn't who I thought he was?" Rage and confusion warred inside Josh. Part of him wanted to strike Ereth again but, in this setting, she did not seem like a threat.

"Not who. What. But that is a discussion for another day."

Todd grabbed Josh by the shoulder. "Don't listen, Josh. You can't believe a word these creatures say."

"English is not my first language," Ereth said. "But I believe you have a word for making blanket statements about a people based on the actions of a few."

Todd's face went red with anger. "Are you calling me a bigot?"

"Enough," Garnet said. "This is not the time. Todd, calm down. Josh, Todd's right about one thing. We have to move. We have too much to do. We can't afford to sit here any longer."

Josh glanced back at the book again. With a sigh, he shook his head. "I'm sorry, Ereth. A part of me truly wants to believe you're telling the truth. Maybe at one point our races coexisted peacefully. But that won't happen now. If the Orpheans and Edimmu appear openly on Earth, war is the only outcome I can see. Our planet can barely sustain the life forms we have now. How can it support another two races?"

Garnet nodded. "And where would you go? I doubt most countries would just give up large pieces of land for you to live. We have so many wars going on already, so many refugees. We can't take anymore."

Ereth spoke slowly, her voice barely audible. "There will be more room than you think. When the device is activated there will be a culling."

"What did you say?" Todd leaned forward, his face only inches away from Ereth. His voice rumbled low with anger.

A bell rang in the hallway, the sound dulled by the closed door.

Josh stood and placed his ear to the door. "Is that the alarm?"

"I'm sorry, children." Ereth crouched down, as if crumpling beneath the weight of Todd's stare. "That is not the alarm. It's a signal. It means the plan of the Council of Peacocks worked. The device has been activated."

Josh's eyes went wide. "No!"

Garnet grabbed Josh's arms. "We can't just sit here. We have to do something."

"There is nothing to be done," Ereth said. "It is too late. Your spirit is half Atlantean. Reach out with your mind and you will feel it. The walls of the Axeinus grow weaker. It is only a matter of time before the first doorway appears."

"You tricked us." Todd punched Ereth in the head. The old Edimmu crumpled, falling against the table. "We were right there. We could have done something to stop this."

Ereth rubbed her cheek where Todd had punched her. "If you had stayed, the only thing you would have accomplished is dying. The Atlantean army numbers 100,000. They would cut you down in seconds. Bringing you here saved your life. There has already been enough senseless death. I saw no reason to add to that number."

Josh covered his fist with telekinetic armor and punched the wall. The stone cracked.

"There's something you're not telling us," Garnet said. "You mentioned a culling and senseless death. What's going to happen?"

Ereth shook her head. "It's not going to happen, child. It already has."

Chapter Thirty-One

Wisdom grabbed Ahriman by the throat. "Show me what you've done."

Still smiling, Ahriman said "My pleasure."

Wisdom felt his consciousness speed out of his body and flow into the mirror behind the throne. He saw through billions of reflective surfaces simultaneously. It wasn't only mirrors. Whatever Ahriman had done allowed Wisdom to see reflections from airplane windows, still lakes, and gleaming satellites. He felt omniscient. The rush of information was exhilarating. And terrifying.

He saw energy rush over the Anomalies in Windsor; saw the looks of terror and confusion on their faces. The device spat forth blinding-white light that blasted up through the ceiling high into the atmosphere.

In an instant, the city of Windsor was leveled. Office towers and homes flattened, people tossed like leaves in the wind. Across the river in Detroit, the windows in skyscrapers shattered, spraying the streets below. The sculpture in Hart Plaza flew up Woodward Avenue. The Ambassador Bridge connecting Canada and America shattered like crystal. Busy at this time of day, hundreds of cars plunged into the Detroit River. No one in those cars escaped alive.

Everyone in the city exposed directly to the energy disintegrated. A few, those underground or at the outskirts of the city, survived. Perhaps the ones that died were the lucky ones. The survivors were...changed.

Wisdom felt his stomach drop. "This is a holocaust. So many dead."

Ahriman laughed. "Oh, silly man. It hasn't even started yet. Keep watching."

Above Windsor, a mushroom cloud formed. It hung high in the air, visible from as far away as Toronto and Chicago. He saw images from newsrooms around both countries as reports came in. Everyone assumed it was a nuclear strike, a terrorist attack. But before the reporters could get on the air, the mushroom cloud exploded, ejecting a stronger wave of bright white light to envelop the entire globe. An electromagnetic pulse followed. Within a minute of the device being activated, the entire world went dark.

Planes fell from the sky. Car engines stopped suddenly, causing innumerable accidents. Computer systems around the world crashed. City streets around the world filled with panicked people. Wisdom watched as nuclear reactors on several continents failed, leaking radioactivity into the surrounding areas.

The atmosphere of the planet pulsed with electricity. Then, light rained down on land and sea. This caused quieter deaths, casualties that could not be blamed on a normal electromagnetic pulse. The power transformed everyone it touched. For the very old and the very young, the exposure proved too much. Their brains exploded near the hypothalamus, killing them.

The sick were erased as well. Whether advanced cancer, AIDS, or pneumonia, everyone with a challenged immune system died.

Wisdom felt the strength fade from his body and he fell to his knees. "Make it stop. Get these visions out my head. This is monstrous."

"Not yet," Ahriman said. "If you stop now you'll miss the best part."

The visions in Wisdom's mind took him to the Arctic Circle. Ice and tundra around the North Pole fell in upon themselves, creating a hole several miles in diameter. A gigantic steam fissure erupted, creating a steamy dome.

"What is that?"

Ahriman stepped off the throne and knelt down beside Wisdom. "That is the first of the really interesting things. The device is recreating a land out of legend. Lemuria."

Wisdom shook his head. "Impossible. Lemuria was in the Pacific Ocean, not the North Pole."

"And that's what makes this so interesting. The device works off the collective unconscious of the planet. If enough people believed it, this device has made it a reality. You've heard the legends of Hyperborea? The silly robots know there is a hole in their history, so they've invented a past. Keep watching. You'll really like this next part."

The Atlantic Ocean churned as an immense continent pushed up from the seafloor, racing towards the sky. It stretched north to the coast of England and south to the Bahamas. The eastern edge could be seen from the Strait of Gibraltar while the western edge formed off the coast of Newfoundland. In the center of this island, surrounded by concentric circles of land and fresh water, stood a city Wisdom had once called home.

"Poseidia. It's just like I remember." Complex emotions rushed through Wisdom. Fear. Hope. Joy. Dread. As he watched, the islands of the Azores became mountaintops. Ships were stranded in the middle of fields. Structures destroyed millennia before, suddenly rebuilt. "That's not possible."

"Oh, but it is. Atlantis rises."

The visions switched to the shorelines of Penglai City on the Bohai Sea, China. Another island, much smaller than Atlantis, rose up from the ocean floor. At its center, a mountain soared to the edge of the clouds. Spiraling up from the mountain were dozens of palaces that gleamed with gold. Pale mist danced along the tops of trees and temples.

"It can't be." Wisdom pulled his hand off Ahriman's throat and the visions faded. "Mount Penglai is only a legend. A myth like Oz or Neverland."

Ahriman rubbed his throat and his eyes grew vacant. "This is the one thing we could not control. The robots controlled the Activation. Almost a third of them are Chinese. We were arrogant to forget the impact they would have. It is only a matter of time before the Eight Immortals appear. And they won't be alone. Who knows what else will be created. The device could create anything if enough robots believe in it."

Wisdom backed away from Ahriman. Every muscle in his body went limp. He realized it was over. Nothing he did could stop this now. Even if he traveled back in time, all he could affect was minor changes. The future of Earth had been changed. All he could do was accept it.

Well, there was one thing he could still do.

Squaring his shoulders, he stared Ahriman in the eyes. "I'm going to kill you."

Ahriman shrugged. "You could try. But there's really no point. What's done is done. So, like I said before, let's discuss what comes next."

Chapter Thirty-Two

Josh went to the door. "We have to get out of here."

Ereth shook her head. "You can't leave. Not that way. The hallways will be flooded with people heading to the exit."

"Well, we can't stay here." Josh pulled Garnet and Todd towards him, huddling together. "Whatever Ereth says, it's not over yet. We can't think that way. We need to get to Wisdom and find a way to stop this."

Garnet's eyes were wide and glossy. "What if it really is too late? If the Orpheans are already heading to Earth, how can we ever hope to stop that?"

Josh lowered his voice. "Last night you convinced me not to give up. Now I'm asking you to do the same thing. I can't accept that everything we've fought for ends with us losing. So we are leaving this room and we are going to stop the armies from reaching Earth."

When Garnet nodded, Josh turned to face Ereth. "Where did they take Wisdom?"

Ereth folded her arms across her chest. "There is a fine line between bravery and insanity. But if I can't convince you to be rational, the least I can do is help you not get yourself killed. They took Wisdom to the parliament building. He is with the leader of the Atlanteans, Ahriman."

"Stop calling them that," Todd said. "They are not Atlanteans. They are Orpheans. Monsters."

Ereth raised an eyebrow. "Some Atlanteans are monsters, yes. But many are normal people. Husbands, daughters, teachers. Are there no humans you would classify as a monster?"

"Orpheans are not people. They are demons."

"Strange," Ereth said. "I assumed you would be relieved to know you do not have demon blood inside you. You are simply partially Atlantean."

"I don't believe your lies." Todd grabbed Ereth's robe, raised a fist as if to hit her again. "We've all seen the evidence. We know a demon when we see one. Now tell us how to get to Wisdom or so help me..."

Josh pushed Todd away from Ereth. "This isn't helping. She's an old woman."

"She's not a woman! She's one of them. A monster."

"Look at her!" Josh grabbed Todd, forcing his head in Ereth's direction. "Whatever she looks like, she's not a threat. And for right now, we need her."

Todd clenched his jaw and stomped off to the far end of the room.

Garnet turned to Ereth. "You say you want to help us. Start giving us some good news. How can we get to Wisdom?"

Ereth pressed a button on the top of the table, and the surface became reflective. Like a mirror. "This is how we travel in the Axeinus. With a minor exertion of power, a mirror can become an effective portal. If you insist on going to Wisdom, I will accompany you. I can get us inside the parliament building but I cannot promise we will ever get out. Follow me."

Ereth placed her hands over the reflective tabletop. Mist-like shadows fell from her fingertips, coating the surface. It fogged over, becoming opaque. Then she wiped a circle clean and jumped into it.

"Whoa," Todd said. "That is some freaky crap."

"Well it's hardly the strangest part about today," Garnet said. She climbed up onto the table and jumped through the opening after Ereth.

"I'm not sure I agree with that." Todd shivered. "This is pretty much the strangest thing I've ever done. It's like something from a Bugs Bunny cartoon."

Josh laughed. "Well, if it's good enough for Elmer Fudd, it's good enough for me. Come on. Let's go after them."

Josh fell through the hole and landed feet-first in shadows. He blinked to help his eyes adjust and moved out of the way so Todd could follow him. Ereth and Garnet crouched behind a stone wall, peering out through a doorway. Garnet raised a finger to her lips, motioning for Josh to be quiet. He crept forward and knelt down beside her. When he looked around the corner, he saw the reason for remaining silent.

Wisdom stood 20 feet away, his hand gripping the throat of the most hideous image Josh had ever seen.

'What the hell is that thing?'

Ereth turned to Josh, projected her thoughts into his mind. 'That is the leader of the Atlanteans, Ahriman.'

Josh cringed. 'Why are you in my head? Won't they sense us talking?"

Ereth shook her head. 'There is nothing unusual about an Edimmu using telepathy in a place like this. As long as you leave me in control of the communication, they won't ever notice we're here.'

Josh took a deep breath, relieved. Then he looked back at the scene before him. 'And we're supposed to believe that is not a demon?'

Ereth looked away. 'He has not always looked like that. Before the Disease took him, you would have thought he looked human.'

Josh forced his eyes away from Ahriman and searched the rest of the area. Row after row of stone pews lined either side of the room. A carpeted aisle led from the gothic archway at the far end to the gilded throne on which Ahriman sat. Above it all, shadows filled the cathedral-high ceiling. Glowing red eyes flittered about in the dark like bats hunting for food.

Josh's father stood to the left of the archway.

Arms crossed, Richard Wilkinson focused on the conversation between Wisdom and Ahriman. His father grinned, a look of triumph plastered on his face.

Josh lost his balance. Legs numb and head spinning, he fell backward. Garnet steadied him. She looked past him and saw Josh's father. Her eyes went wide and she tightened her grip on his arm. Josh hung his head as tears formed in his eyes.

'I came here to kill him,' he thought. 'But now that I see him…Can I do this? Can I really kill my father?'

Looking up, he studied the man before him. He knew that face so well. Hours spent training after school. Small talk over dinners. Smiles at Christmas. Singing in the car. How did all those memories relate to the monster who had killed his mother?

Ereth touched his shoulder. 'I feel your rage, child, but this is not the time. Approach your father now and Ahriman will strike you down.'

"I don't care!" Too late, Josh realized he'd spoken aloud.

Wisdom turned and looked directly at Josh. He winked once and turned back to face Ahriman.

Ereth's voice entered Josh's mind again. 'Even if Wisdom can stop Ahriman, Richard Wilkinson is a very powerful man, a high-ranking member of the Council of Peacocks. Do you know what he is capable of?'

An image flashed across Josh's mind: blood-stained carpet, an overturned couch, a pale body with charred clothes.

Fists clenched, he turned to Ereth. 'I know what he's capable of. That's why I have to do this.'

Before anyone could stop him, Josh stood up and walked across the room towards his father.

***

As soon as Josh stood, Wisdom stopped controlling his rage. Reaching behind, Wisdom grabbed mental control of the stone floor. He reshaped it, lifting it up to create a barrier of rock separating the others from him and Ahriman.

Ahriman's leathery wings flared up behind him. "Fighting me is futile. You've already lost the war. You just refuse to accept it."

Wisdom smirked. "Well, I've always been stubborn." Fingers outstretched, he briefly opened a portal the size of a quarter. It connected with the surface of the sun. For a millisecond, a thin stream of superheated plasma seared through the air, too fast for Ahriman to dodge. It struck the Orphean in the chest, burning a tunnel directly through his body. It continued on, eating away at the walls of the throne room.

There was a rush of air as the fire ate up the oxygen in the room. With an exertion of will, Wisdom opened a portal to the elemental plane of air and replaced the atmosphere.

"I'm not that easy to kill." Ahriman placed a hand over the hole in his chest. Shadows bled from his fingertips, filling the wound. Flesh began to re-knit.

"Neither am I." Wisdom opened a larger teleportation disk and fell. He reappeared behind Ahriman and punched him in the back. The Orphean flew forward, slamming into the stone wall Wisdom had created. "I don't care if the device was activated or not. You will never leave the Axeinus."

Above, the creatures in shadows squealed.

Ahriman pushed himself away from the wall and wiped dust off the edges of his wings. "You're wrong, Wisdom. I will lead my people back to their homeland. There's nothing you can do to stop it. You, on the other hand, are stuck here. You really should have left with your father."

"The djinn is not my father."

"Don't quibble. He cared about you, which is why he told you to go home. Or did you forget why you had to leave Earth?"

Wisdom hesitated. Months ago, before their final battle, the djinn had told Wisdom he couldn't stay on Earth. But it was only after a conversation with Defksquar that he understood why. The device would weaken all barriers between dimensions, not only the ones to the Axeinus. All they need is an anchor. For the Orpheans, that was the Anomalies. If Wisdom returned to Earth, he would be an anchor to the realm of the djinn. It was the reason Defksquar didn't activate the device himself. His alien DNA would have polluted the Earth.

The fire in Wisdom's eyes died.

Ahriman chuckled. "Ah. It finally sinks in."

"My father was an isolationist. He had a very tenuous grasp on a minor position of power. He worried that if I remained on Earth when the device was activated, djinn would swarm the Earth. Worse, it could create new djinn native to Earth."

Ahriman folded his wings and walked towards Wisdom. "All my people want is freedom. We will go to our homeland in peace. But the djinn? You spent thousands of years with them. What do you think they'll do to your precious humans?"

Wisdom lifted his hand and covered his mouth. He saw his hand shaking but could not stop it.

"You could be lying," he said. "Or wrong. You can't know what will happen if I head back. I make it a rule never to trust the bad guys."

"Bad guy?" Ahriman held up his hands, palms outward, a sign of surrender. "You think I'm the bad guy? How quaint. We both know there's no such thing as bad guys. Good and evil are simply a matter of perspective. All I'm doing is fighting for the safety and security of my people. To them, I'm a hero. A savior. If I'm the villain in your story, you are the villain in mine."

Wisdom took a deep breath. "Keep telling yourself that. Whatever helps you sleep at night. You violated hundreds of humans to create the Anomalies. Orpheans have fed on misery, forced people into monstrous acts. And now? You just murdered millions of people because you want a bigger house. I don't believe that good and evil are matters of perspective. Not anymore. I've lived a very long time. For most of my life, I've been cowardly and selfish. I've done…unspeakable things. Things I can't take back, things for which I'll never be forgiven. I know what evil is, and I'm looking at it right now. Maybe you're right. Maybe I can't ever return to Earth. But you're forgetting something else."

Wisdom looked behind Ahriman's throne at the massive mirrors the Orphean used to show him the effects of the Activation.

Ahriman followed Wisdom's gaze. "Where do you plan on going? No section of Earth is open to you, no matter how remote."

"Are you still talking?" Wisdom shot a blast of fire at Ahriman. When the Orphean dodged, Wisdom opened a portal directly in Ahriman's path. He closed the portal. The Orphean was gone.

Wisdom walked to the mirror. His fingers traced the surface as he studied his reflection.

He knew what he had to do.

***

As Josh walked towards his father, the expression on Richard Wilkinson's face changed rapidly. When he first saw Josh, his eyes bulged and he lowered his body into a fighter's stance. Then he smiled, eyes warm and welcoming. Just as quickly as the smile appeared, it was gone. Richard Wilkinson closed his eyes and turned away, letting his shoulders sag.

Josh felt a flutter of nerves in his stomach but did not stop walking until he stood directly in front of his father.

For a moment, silence.

Richard opened his eyes. "I had to. Everything I've done was for a reason."

Josh punched his father in the head. Or he tried to. Richard easily side-stepped the blow and pushed Josh off balance. Josh fell to the ground but quickly rolled to his feet.

"I can't let you kill me," Richard said. "I know you want to. Maybe I deserve it. But the Council of Peacocks just saved the world. There was a price."

"Bastard!" Josh dropped his telekinetic armor and drove his power at his father's chest. This time he didn't miss. Richard flew back through the archway. The Edimmu guards turned to Josh, spears lowered.

"No," his father said as he got back to his feet. "He's my son. My son! I will take care of this. Go be with the others. We'll be leaving soon."

Hot tears flooded Josh's eyes. He wiped them away with clenched fists.

Richard waited for the Edimmu to leave before speaking. "You can't beat me, Josh. I trained you. Just calm down and let me…"

"Calm down?" Josh grabbed one of the pews with his mind and threw it at his father. Richard dodged the attack. "Calm down? You killed my mother. Butchered her. I saw…" He couldn't finish the sentence. The image, the emotion was too raw.

Richard took a step closer to Josh. "If I didn't do it, someone else would have. It was always part of the plan. Her death was the distraction we…"

"Distraction?" Josh reached out with his mind again. This time, two pews rose in the air. "Did you just call my mother's death a distraction?"

"Enough!" Richard waved his hands and the pews crashed back to the floor. "Do you think this has been easy for me? I loved your mother."

"Bull! You don't kill people you love."

"Life is more complex than that. And thanks to me, you'll live long enough to find out."

Josh narrowed his eyes. "What do you mean?"

Richard smiled and looked around the room. "This is the one place I knew you'd be safe. By now, Earth is in complete chaos. Millions dead or dying. Luring you here was the only way to…"

Josh jumped forward, calling up his telekinetic armor. He punched his father in the chest. Not expecting the blow, Richard was unable to dodge it and flew back. Before he hit the ground, Josh dropped his armor and mentally grabbed his father by the waist. He threw his father just as he'd thrown the pews. Richard slammed into a wall. Before Richard could recover, Josh struck, pinning him to the ground.

"You didn't lure me here," Josh said. "We found out about your plan all on our own."

Richard cleared his throat but did not try to get to his feet. "And that didn't strike you as convenient? Learning about the plot just as it was about to unfold? Come on, Josh. I taught you better than that."

Josh swallowed and shook his head. "I don't buy it. There's no way you could have planned for this. How did you know we'd find a way into the Axeinus?"

"Ahriman has eyes everywhere. Literally. Orpheans use mirrors like cameras. They see everything."

Josh punched his father in the head. "Did they see that?"

Richard grunted as he was knocked unconscious.

"Josh?"

Looking over, he saw Todd approaching him. "Stay out of this. It's between me and my father."

"Fine by me," Todd said. "But you might want to turn around. Something's happened to Wisdom. Look."

Still pinning his father in place, Josh twisted around. The walls Wisdom had built were slowly disintegrating. Wisdom stood alone. There was no sign of Ahriman. Above, all the red glowing eyes were disappearing, fading back into the shadows.

"What happened?" Josh asked. "Is that creature dead?"

Todd shook his head. "I don't know. But we should find out."

Josh looked down at his father. "I can't just leave him here."

Todd knelt down beside Josh. "I've got this. I'm inside his windpipe. If he moves, he won't be breathing for long."

Josh shivered. "When did you get so scary?"

"A few hours ago. Now, go to Wisdom."

Nodding, Josh stood and walked towards the mirror behind the throne.

***

Wisdom saw movement out of the corner of his eye. He glanced over and found Josh beside him.

"Is he gone?" Josh asked.

Wisdom sighed. "Not for long."

"Where did you send him?"

"To the village we went through when we first arrived here. He fought against the teleportation. No one else has ever been able to do that. He won't be gone long." Wisdom massaged the tension from his neck. "Look, Josh, things didn't go exactly as planned. In fact, I can't imagine them being any worse. The Council's plan worked. Look."

Josh cleared his throat. "My cousin, Travis, is he…?"

"I don't know."

Josh looked at the mirror. His eyes went wide as the mirror's surface faded and he saw the Orphean armies flooding out of the dimensional rift. The Turkish army engaged them but it was obviously not a fair fight.

"Dear God," Josh said. "It's a slaughter. Where's Ms. Ryerson?"

Wisdom lowered his head. "I can't find her. But it's worse than this. Josh, we lost. Your cousin activated the device. Ahriman showed me."

Josh took a step back. "Travis. Is he…?"

"I don't know."

"And the others? David? Elaine? Jessica?"

Wisdom closed his eyes for a moment. When he reopened them, he watched as the color bled from Josh's face. His eyes flickered for a moment before he turned away, staring at the ground.

Wisdom sighed. "I'm not sure. Ahriman used mirrors to create visual connections with many places around the world. He was gloating, showing me what the device did to our planet. The world changed in an instant. It's complete chaos out there. But the device released so much energy that it broke Ahriman's connection. Maybe your cousin and the others are fine. Maybe not. But I need you to listen. Just for a few minutes. Promise me not to panic."

Josh nodded and wiped tears from his eyes. "Fine. I'm listening."

Wisdom looked down at his hands. His fingers were shaking. "It's funny. I haven't had to be brave in so long. When I was a kid, I was afraid all the time. The djinn beat me, tore my soul apart. When I came back to Earth, my fear became rage. Anger fueled me for centuries. But for what I have to do next, I need something other than rage and fear. I need to be very, very brave."

"I don't understand."

Wisdom grabbed Josh by the shoulders, forcing him to look directly into Wisdom's eyes. "I have to go away, Josh. I'm going somewhere far away and I'm not sure if I'll ever be able to come back."

"No!" Garnet shouted the word as she ran from her hiding spot. Wisdom was surprised to see a female Edimmu with her.

"Don't make this any harder than it is." Wisdom swallowed, his throat thick with emotion.

"We need you here," Garnet said. "If the Council won, if they really did activate that device, the world needs you more than ever."

"Maybe it does," Wisdom said as he looked back at the mirrors. "But it can't have me. The barriers that form reality on Earth are fragile. Mutable. As soon as one Orphean set foot on Earth, all barriers around the Axeinus fell. The demons are now free to walk beyond the Black Sea. If I step foot on Earth, the same thing will happen to the barriers that keep the djinn locked within the Kaz. My father was one of the minor djinn. He alone could have destroyed the world. There are millions of djinn in the Kaz, most of them significantly more powerful than my father. Millions. I can't let them have free reign on Earth."

"So, what?" Garnet said. "You're just going to stay here?"

Josh stared at the mirrors behind the throne. "No. He said he was going away. You're going to Maghe Sihre, aren't you?"

Wisdom raised an eyebrow. "Either that was a good guess or your psychic abilities are growing."

Josh laughed.

Garnet hit Josh in the shoulder. "Don't encourage him. Wisdom, you can't leave. I won't let you."

Wisdom touched Garnet's cheek. Leaning in, he kissed her on the forehead. "I'm so proud of you, Garnet. You have come so far from the little cat burglar I found in Vancouver. Stop fighting me. I may not be right all the time, but this time I know I am. You and Josh are the only Anomalies I know for certain are still alive and fighting the good fight. The rest are either dead or they've been turned into monsters by the Council. I need you two to find Ms. Ryerson. I saw her fall on the battlefield but she's just as hard to kill as I am. Once you have her, head back to my offices in New York. My resources are yours now. Ms. Ryerson can introduce you to Penny Dulany. She's an old friend, you can trust her. She has access to the Illuminati. Let them know what happened here. Use them. Do whatever good you can."

Nodding, Josh extended his hand. Wisdom grasped it firmly and shook it.

Garnet threw herself against Wisdom, hugging him tightly. "I will not say goodbye because you are going to come back."

Wisdom pushed Garnet away gently. "I'm afraid that may not be an option."

"Why Maghe Sihre?" Josh asked.

Wisdom took a deep breath. "Well, I'm not going back to the Kaz. And Maghe Sihre sure as hell beats staying here. I hope. Besides, maybe I can track down our friend with the gold ring, Defksquar. None of this would have happened without him. I plan on making him pay for what he's done."

Wisdom looked back at the archway. Todd stood above an unmoving Richard Wilkinson.

"I couldn't do it," Josh said. "Once I knocked him out I tried to kill him, but I…Maybe I'm not as cold as I thought I was."

Wisdom smiled. "That may be the best news of the day. Keep a tight hold on your humanity, Josh. You will need it more than ever in this new world."

Turning his back on the others, Wisdom placed his hands on the mirrors and copied the energetic manipulations he'd watched Ahriman perform earlier. The mirror became a portal, a doorway similar to his teleportation disk. The benefit of mirror travel was that it did not require him to tear his body apart into energy form. It also allowed him to travel further. He set an image in his mind of the only place in Maghe Sihre he knew: the forest where he'd met Defksquar.

Slowly, the mirror fogged over. Once completely opaque, Wisdom wiped it clean with his hands. The sensation was odd, cold and wet. With each swipe of his hand, the scene became clearer. Tall trees rose high in the air, creating a tranquil clearing filled with dappled sunlight.

"Wisdom!" Garnet shouted his name. "Wait. There's so much we don't know."

He turned to look back at her. "Thankfully, I took good notes. Josh, you know where to look for those notes, right?"

Josh hesitated for a moment before nodding.

"Smart boy." Wisdom turned toward the mirror. Then he stopped and looked around sharply at Josh. "Promise me, no matter what you read, no matter what happens, stay off the moon."

Josh raised his eyebrows. "Come again?"

"You heard me." Wisdom looked around one last time and let out a long, slow breath. "Suddenly, I don't really want to go."

Before he could change his mind, Wisdom stepped through the mirror portal and was gone.

Chapter Thirty-Three

Josh watched Wisdom step through the mirror. An instant later, the mirror fogged over again. The mist dissipated slowly and the mirror's surface was once again reflective.

Garnet grabbed Josh by the forearms. "What was he talking about? What's on the moon?"

Josh threw his hands up. "Don't ask me. I have no flippin' clue. Besides, we have more important concerns right now."

They walked over to Todd and told him what had happened.

"Well, damn," Todd said. "What the hell are we supposed to do now?"

Josh ran his fingers through his hair. "We don't stop. Wisdom is gone but the fight continues. We need to get to Ms. Ryerson. Ereth, what's the fastest way out of here?"

"The walls of the Axeinus are falling," she answered. "There are seven Atlantean teleportation devices set up throughout this dimension. If things are moving on schedule, half the population should already be on Earth."

Garnet shook her head. "We can't just walk out with them. Josh, maybe we should head back to the gate we took to get here."

Todd groaned. "That's a truly horrible idea. That's where Wisdom sent Ahriman, remember?"

Josh glanced at the mirror. "What about that? Ereth, can you help us travel through the mirror?"

"Perhaps." Ereth squinted her eyes. Her forked, reptilian tongue slipped out of her mouth, a movement that repulsed Josh.

"How does it work?" Todd walked to the mirror and ran his hands over the surface. "Please tell me this is a special type of mirror."

Ereth shook her head. "There is magic in all reflective surfaces. Glass, water, gems, polished stone. The cleaner the reflection, the easier to use."

Todd shivered. "So the Orpheans could teleport into any place with a mirror?"

Ereth spoke with in a calm, reassuring tone. "Not quite. Scrying is easy but the barriers prevented Orpheans from traveling physically through mirrors. Humans and Edimmu could come and go freely but the Atlanteans were trapped. They could, however, send their astral bodies, their shadows, through the mirrors. If they wanted to stay on Earth, they needed to find a body they could posses."

Todd's jaw dropped. "Is that supposed to make me feel better?"

Garnet crossed her arms across her chest and focused on the mirror. "By scrying, you mean seeing things from a distance, right?"

Ereth nodded.

Garnet's face lit up. "Can you show us where Ms. Ryerson is?"

"I can try." Ereth closed her eyes. "Open your mind to me and think of the person you seek. I will search for her."

Josh watched as Garnet closed her eyes. A flicker of power flowed over Ereth's body. The shadows in the room darkened and the mirror's surfaced changed. Instead of a reflection of the room, the mirror became a window looking out onto a battlefield. An unending stream of Orpheans covered in shadow armor streamed by. Flashes of light – bullet trails – bounced off their armor. Edimmu pointed their spears at Turkish soldiers, shooting deadly bolts of blue electricity. Behind them, the night sky erupted in silent explosions. Josh searched the chaos for a sign of Ms. Ryerson.

"There she is." Todd pointed at the edge of a tent. Ms. Ryerson knelt on the ground, holding her arm. It was bent at an unnatural angle.

"We have to get to her," Garnet said. "Open the portal now."

Ereth shook her head. "We're watching this scene through the reflective surface of a car's front window. The reflective surface is not strong enough for travel, only for scrying. I'll search for a connection strong enough for us to travel through."

"Be quick. Ahriman could be back any second." Josh looked to the far end of the room. His father still lay unconscious beneath the archway. "We'll have to take my father, too. I can't kill him but I'm definitely not letting him out of my sight."

"We can turn him over to Candleworks," Garnet said. "Remember those holding cells they showed us in Ottawa?"

Josh nodded. Last month, to help foster a better working relationship with Wisdom, Candleworks had given them a guided tour of their facilities. Josh had met several agents including a man named Gabriel, the agent hired to replace his father. Gabriel had shown them a basement level filled with special prison cells designed to hold Anomalies and Edimmu.

"Good plan," Josh said. "They have more experience dealing with prisoners than we do. But, first things first. Ereth, work your magic. Get us out of here."

Josh pointed towards his father. "Todd, can you give me hand?" Todd followed Josh back to the archway. They each threw one of Richard Wilkinson's arms over their shoulders and dragged him across the room. As they lifted him up the steps and behind the throne, Ereth moved her fingers over the mirror, tracing complex symbols in the air.

"Your friend, Wisdom, made this look very easy," Ereth said. "I've never seen someone open a portal that quickly. He must be incredibly powerful."

Garnet bit her lip and looked away. "Wisdom is one of a kind. Can anyone travel this way?"

Ereth narrowed her eyes as she looked at Garnet. She shook her head. "Anyone can learn the basics of magic with enough training and dedication. Opening a portal like this requires a great deal of concentration and willpower. Most mortals – Atlantean, human, or Edimmu – simply cannot focus that well. You, however, are strong enough. If we had the time I could train you." Ereth looked back at the mirror. "Speaking of focus…"

Garnet smiled. "Of course. I'll let you work."

Agonizing minutes passed. Finally, Ereth sighed, a sound of pure exhaustion.

"I found one," she said. "There's a full-length mirror in a tent not far from the battlefield."

Josh watched as, once again, the mirror fogged over. Ereth wiped it clear, revealing a vacant, dimly lit tent. A small bed stood at one end. It was the only piece of furniture in the room. An open suitcase stood on the floor nearby.

"Hurry," Ereth said. "I can feel Ahriman. He's approaching very quickly. We don't have much time."

Garnet pushed ahead first. "You don't have to tell me twice. I've only seen that creature once and once was more than enough."

Todd took Richard Wilkinson's arm off his shoulder and, kneeling down, grabbed Richard's feet. Josh took the full weight of his father's shoulders. Then they stepped, single file, through the mirror. Ereth entered last.

Josh turned back and watched as the mirror fogged over again. The sound of something exploding nearby reminded him they had avoided one battle only to land in another.

Ereth pushed aside the tent flap. "Your friend, Ms. Ryerson, is in this direction. Leave your father with me. Go straight to the next tent and then turn right."

Todd hesitated. "You're not coming with us?"

Ereth shook her head. "It's best I stay here. You may run into Edimmu. You do not want to make me choose between helping you and helping my people. Get your friend and come back here. I'll work on finding us an escape route."

Josh touched Ereth's shoulder, a gesture of thanks. "We owe you our lives. It's a debt I will not forget."

Ereth smiled and looked at the ground. "I fear if you meet my people out there they will not be as generous as I've been. We are slaves, yes, but some of us have learned to love our enslavers. May the gods grant you speed."

Josh nodded and ran out into the battle.

Chapter Thirty-Four

Josh crouched behind a tent and looked out at the warzone before him. 'This is insane. How am I going to find Ms. Ryerson in all this chaos?'

Human soldiers fired automatic weapons at the sky. An Edimmu flew past one soldier, grabbed him by the shoulders and lifted him into the sky. A moment later, the soldier's body dropped onto a nearby parked Jeep, smashing the windshield.

Following Ereth's instructions, he turned left and walked between rows of identical tents. An Edimmu flew above him. Josh clenched his fists and readied his telekinetic armor. Blazing light struck the Edimmu midflight, knocking it off course. Its body erupted in flames as the Edimmu crashed into a tent in the distance.

'What the hell was that? A bazooka?' Josh slapped his face. 'Snap out of it, Josh. No time to focus on that. Get to Ms. Ryerson and get out of here. This is not your battle.'

Keeping low, Josh forced himself to keep going. Something stirred in the shadows ahead. His heart beat faster, preparing him for a battle. Then he recognized the shadow and relaxed his armor.

"Ms. Ryerson. It's Josh." Kneeling beside her, he touched her neck. She turned to look up at him. Blood covered half her face; the other half was burned, blackened, and charred.

"Josh," she said. "What are you doing here? Where's Wisdom?"

Josh shook his head. "I'll tell you later. We need to get out of here. Can you move?"

Ms. Ryerson looked down at her legs. Josh followed her eyes and noticed both legs were twisted like her arm.

Ms. Ryerson turned away. "There were more than we expected. So many more. They came so fast. Most of the Turkish army is still on their way here."

Josh looked up as another Edimmu flew above him. "It'll be too late by then. Okay, I'm going to try to carry you. I'll be as gentle as I can but it's going to hurt."

Ms. Ryerson grimaced. "I can deal with pain. Just get me out of here."

He slipped his hands beneath Ms. Ryerson and, using his telekinesis for extra strength, lifted her wounded body close to his chest. It was impossible to crouch and carry her at the same time. Standing tall, he headed back towards the tent where Garnet and the others waited.

"You're heading the wrong way," Ms. Ryerson said. "This will take us closer to the fighting."

"Trust me. I've got a way out."

An Edimmu flew above then. This time it saw Josh. Turning midair, it landed on the ground a few feet in front of them. Hissing, it flared its wings and crouched low to attack. As it charged, Ms. Ryerson extended her hand. A blast of wind appeared out of nowhere. It caught the Edimmu's wings, pushing it up and back. It landed in a tent and quickly became twisted in the material.

"How many powers do you have?" Josh looked down at Ms. Ryerson.

"Just one but many ways to use it." Ms. Ryerson coughed and her face contorted with pain. "Put me down. The Edimmu is coming back. You need your hands to fight him.

As gently as he could, Josh placed Ms. Ryerson down and turned back to face the Edimmu. It tore through the tent with sharp claws and screamed in rage. Turning towards Josh, it spat forth a blast of solid shadow. Josh extended his telekinetic armor out in front of him, creating a force-field. The shadow blast splashed over the shield like water. The force pushed Josh back but he stood his ground. When the blast stopped, Josh ran as quickly as he could straight at the Edimmu. Claws slashed at Josh, bouncing off his shield. He punched the Edimmu in the chest. Its black armor cracked, the bones snapping so loudly Josh heard them even over the sound of battle.

Before the Edimmu could attack again, Josh lowered his shield, grabbed the Edimmu's right arm, and then formed his shield again. Only Josh was protected by the shield. When it reformed, it sliced right through the Edimmu's arm, cutting it off at the elbow. The Edimmu screamed in pain. Blood splattered against Josh's shield. He dropped the dismembered arm and punched the Edimmu in the jaw, driving it to the ground. When it fell, Josh brought his boots down repeatedly on the creature's head. He didn't stop until the skull was flat.

He rushed to pick up Ms. Ryerson and continued to the tent.

"Neat trick," Ms. Ryerson said. "Where'd you learn it?"

Josh groaned. "From you."

"That's right. I told you it would come in handy one day."

"Useful but super gross. I hope I never have to do that again."

Ms. Ryerson reached out and touched Josh's face. "I'm afraid you'll have to do much worse than that in the days ahead. Where is Wisdom? Is he close?"

Josh looked away. "No. He's gone. Look, our way out is just ahead. I'll explain everything when we're safe. I promise."

Ms. Ryerson's hand fell away. "If Wisdom is gone, than all is lost. We can't fight these creatures on our own."

Josh swallowed, his throat suddenly very dry. "We'll have to find a new way to fight. We don't have a choice."

When Josh ducked back into the tent, Garnet and Todd rushed to him.

"Is she alive?" Todd asked.

"I'm right here," Ms. Ryerson said. "I'm injured, not deaf. Now how are we getting out of here?"

Garnet stepped aside, giving Ms. Ryerson full view of Ereth, who stood beside the mirror.

"You're working with one of them?" Ms. Ryerson's voice was filled with anger and fear.

"Long story," Josh said. "But yes. For now. She's agreed to get us to safety and it's not like we have tons of other options. Ereth, can you open the portal now? The fighting is getting closer."

Ereth nodded and turned back to the mirror. As it began to fog over, Ms. Ryerson closed her eyes.

"Don't you dare fall asleep," Josh said. "We've already lost Wisdom. We can't lose you, too."

Weakly, Ms. Ryerson elbowed Josh in the chest. "I'm not an idiot, child. This is not me falling asleep. This is me focusing on the surroundings to make sure there are no Edimmu nearby." She looked up at Ereth. "Well, no other Edimmu."

The mirror was completely fogged over now.

Ereth turned to face them. "So where will you go?"

"To Wisdom's offices in New York," Josh said. "That's where he wanted us to go. Can you get us there?"

Ereth nodded again. "Normally, Wisdom's buildings are shielded from this type of travel. For some reason, the wards are down." Ereth wiped the mist from the mirror, revealing a large bathroom with multiple stalls. A janitor was plunging one of the toilets.

Garnet went to the mirror first. "What about you, Ereth?"

"I won't be long behind you. Once you've all been transported, I'm heading to the colony in South America. It's time to join my family. Staying here won't be any better for me than for you."

Garnet stepped through the mirror. Josh watched as she climbed over the sink on the other side. The janitor screamed and ran away.

Todd, carrying Richard Wilkinson, went next. Before he left, he turned to Ereth. He could not look her in the eyes. "Thank you. Maybe I was wrong about your kind."

"We're not all monsters," Ereth said. "But some of us are. Beware the soldiers."

Todd nodded and stepped through the mirror.

Ms. Ryerson's eyes were glued to Ereth. "Why are you helping us?"

Ereth looked down. "The Atlanteans think both our people are beneath them. We are slaves. You are tools. Maybe it is time for the Edimmu to find a new ally."

Josh carried Ms. Ryerson to the portal. "Will you be in trouble for helping us?"

Ereth smiled and put her index finger in front of her lips, motioning for silence. "Only if I'm caught. Which I don't intend to. You are still as remarkable as I remember, Josh. The times ahead will be dark. Maybe they will be a bit brighter because you are alive."

Josh shrugged at the compliment. "Thanks. I've learned a lot from you in a short time, Ereth. Take care of yourself." Then he stepped through the portal.

Chapter Thirty-Five

It began quietly. First, there was another soft click that made the soles of their feet vibrate. The five exchanged wary looks with one another, as if to say "Is that it?" There was a hushed moment that hung on the edge of eternity, a pin waiting to drop. Then the Verdenstab erupted, spewing forth radiant white energy with the force of a nuclear bomb.

Travis felt every bone in his body shatter as the energy slammed into him. The light blinded him and he screamed in pain. Just as quickly, his body reformed, now an amalgamation of his old body, the power of the Verdenstab and the fuse he had been holding.

Energy poured forth for what seemed hours. When it stopped, Travis opened his eyes and found he could not see.

'I'm blind!' He opened his mouth to scream but no sound came out. He reached around, panicked. His fingers connected with warm flesh.

"Relax," Iggy said. "It's over. We're alive. Can you talk?"

Travis shook his head. Slowly the white flare over his eyes faded. He saw shadows, movement. He assumed the blob of darkness before him was Iggy.

"That was insane." This voice seemed to be from the one called David. It was further away and Travis could not distinguish which shadow was his. "Travis, you can't see it, but the blast tore out the ceiling. It burned up through the atmosphere. We can see it dancing in the clouds, like the Aurora Borealis or something."

"Plus we're all naked." This was the little girl, Jessica. "Which is totally disgusting. Don't look at me, David, or I swear I'll burn your eyes out."

Travis blinked. The light faded more and he could see colors. He looked down, trying to focus on his hands. The skin was raw but he didn't seem to be missing any body parts.

"We should get out of here." A woman's voice. Elaine. "We can't know for sure if the blast destroyed that creature or not. Even if it is, we should get out of here before the authorities arrive. For something this big, they'll send in the army. Is everyone alright?"

Someone grabbed Travis' shoulder. When he spoke, Travis realized it was Iggy. "I think he's blind. He can't seem to speak, either."

"And, hello, we're all naked." Jessica's voice was filled with disdain. "Why didn't those fuses protect our clothes, too?"

"We're alive," David said. Then he lowered his voice. "Which is probably more than I can say for the other people in the mine."

"Feel sorry for them later," Elaine said. "Look for a way for us to climb out."

Travis rubbed his eyes. Slowly, they were working again. He watched as Elaine turned to study the walls around them. His eyes fell on the Verdenstab. It pulsed with white-blue energy, sending out visible waves of power. He looked up and saw the lights in the clouds. Now that he could see, he looked down at himself to confirm he was uninjured. That's when he noticed something else.

"What happened to the rings?" His throat was raw, the words raspy, but it got everyone's attention.

David looked down at his own hand. "Mine's gone too."

Iggy glanced at his hand briefly. "Maybe they absorbed the power this thing created and disintegrated. Not my biggest concern right now. We need to get out of here. Find someplace safe."

David clenched his fists. "There's no way out. Everything is too jagged to risk climbing. I could fly myself out, look around for a rope or something to throw down to you."

"Sure, David. You're just looking for any excuse to show off your fancy new powers." Jessica crossed her arms over her chest. "Big deal. You can fly. So can I."

A sheath of blue energy wrapped around Jessica. Her eyes went wide, revealing she wasn't consciously doing this. Then she flew up through the air quickly, screaming all the way.

Elaine rushed over to where Jessica had been standing. "You've got to be kidding me. Has anyone ever seen her do something like that before?"

David shook his head. "I've seen her float in the air before but nothing like that. I'll fly after her. It's not like a ladder is going to fall from the sky or anything."

A ladder fell from the sky.

David shrieked, jumping back from the ladder. "What the serious hell was that?"

"Did you do that?" Travis stood and went to the ladder. He touched it to make sure it was real.

"Hell no." David looked at the sky. "I missed out on the spontaneous-laddering-making power. Watch out. Other things might fall."

Elaine picked up the ladder. "However it got here, we have it now. Luckily it's just long enough to reach that overhang there." She pointed to a section of the floor above. "We climb up one level at a time if we need to."

Travis looked at the ladder, then back to his hand. "I think I know where the ladder came from. David, won't it be great if clothes dropped out the sky, too?"

David chuckled. "Yeah, Travis. Because clothing falls from the sky all the time."

Five sets of mining overalls fell from the level above them.

David shrieked again.

Elaine grabbed Travis by the arm and pulled him around. "You know something. Tell me! Did something happen to David?"

Travis inhaled slowly. "I think it happened to all of us. I don't think the rings disintegrated. I think they became part of us." He held up his hand for her to see. "Look closely at the finger I had the ring on. Notice anything different?"

Without releasing his arm, Elaine studied his fingers. Her eyes went wide and she looked down at her own hand. Just like Travis, a thin line of color wrapped around one of her fingers. "I have one too," she said. "The color's different. Mine is black, like the ring I wore."

"What are you talking about?" Iggy came over to look at Travis' hand. When he saw the mark, he looked at his own fingers. "Crap. I have one, too. What does it mean? Was there anything about this happening in that book you read?"

"There was a book?" Elaine asked.

Travis nodded. "It's in the backpack. No way of knowing where it is now. The explosion could have knocked it anywhere."

"It's over there." Iggy pointed at the backpack. It was in exactly the same place Travis had placed it before the activation. "Weird. Why didn't it move?"

Travis shook his head. "We can look for answers after we get out of here. Let's put those suits on before we climb the ladder."

"Good idea." Elaine grabbed a set of overalls and put them on quickly. "On the bright side, at least this day can't get any worse."

A shadow passed overhead, momentarily blocking out the light from the energy in the sky.

"Did you see that?" Travis looked up through the hole. "Did anyone see what it was?"

Everyone shook their heads.

"Jessica's out there by herself." David dressed quickly, repeatedly watching the sky. "I should fly up to get her."

Elaine put the ladder in place. "Where would you look for her? We don't know how far she flew. Jessica can take care of herself. We have no idea what to expect out there. We stick together."

Travis grabbed a set of overalls. After putting them on, he retrieved the backpack and swung it over his shoulder. Everyone dressed quickly. David grabbed the extra set of overalls, carrying it for Jessica. They used the ladder to climb to the next level. Once everyone reached the second level, Elaine pulled the ladder up. Floor by floor, they climbed to the surface. Travis was the first out. He looked around, catching his first full sight of the devastation.

"What have I done?" The ground around the activation site was warped. The concrete road had melted, warped and re-solidified. Now it resembled burnt plastic. All the buildings, trees, and cars were gone, blown away by the blast. He looked north, across the river at Detroit. The skyscrapers of downtown were demolished.

"It took out the bridge, too." Iggy stood behind Travis. His voice was low and pained. "I have a bad feeling, Travis. I think we made a mistake activating that device."

Travis shook his head. "It felt like the right thing to do. I was so sure. Maybe Defksquar lied to me."

"Ya think?" Elaine, the last out of the hole, pulled the ladder up. "That's what he does. He lied to your cousin. That's what I was trying to tell you. You've ruined the world!"

David squealed. "Oh my god, Elaine. Your hands."

"What about them?" Elaine raised her hands in front of her face. Both were surrounded with a cloud of black energy. Panicked, she looked over at Travis. "What the hell have you done to me?"

David touched Elaine's shoulder gently. "We'll figure it out later. What's done is done. Let's find Jessica and get out of here."

The tension on Elaine's face melted at David's touch. She stared at her hands. A moment later, the energy dissipated, her hands returning to normal.

Iggy looked at his own hands. "I'm starting to see a pattern here. Jessica and Elaine show evidence of powers they didn't have before. David wishes for things and they appear. Does that mean I'm going to get superpowers? Because, just saying, best news of the day."

Elaine stared at the horizon. "I don't want superpowers. I want to be human. We have to get out of here. After we find Jessica, I suggest we head for the edge of town. Find a way to contact Wisdom. Hopefully he was more successful with his mission. We need to find what's happened to us, what's happened to the world. If we're lucky, what we see is the extent of the damage. If not, the world as we know it is over. "

A shadow passed over them again. Travis looked up in time to see something impossible.

Iggy looked up as well. "That's a pretty big bird."

A shiver ran through Travis' body. "That's not a bird. That's a…."

"Dragon!" Jessica screamed as she ran to join them. "Run. There's a freaking dragon in the sky!"

"There's no such thing as…." Elaine, looking up, stopped midsentence.

David threw the remaining jumpsuit to Jessica, who wrapped it quickly around her body.

Travis swallowed and shook himself out of the daze. "Jessica, did you see any place we could hide? Any buildings still standing?"

Jessica pointed. "The closest building is that way but it's really far away. We need to run before the thing comes back."

"Too late."

Travis turned at the sound of David's voice and looked up. The creature hovered above them. Sky-blue scales covered its body. Fiery and furious eyes focused directly on Travis.

"Move!" David pushed Travis aside and pointed his hands at the creature. A jet of red flame shot from David's hand. The creature flew up and to the side, easily avoiding the attack. It opened its mouth and spat something down on them.

Jessica jumped in front of David and raised her hands above her head. Green liquid bounced off an invisible shield several feet above them. Travis wasn't so lucky. He felt pain unlike anything he'd ever felt. He screamed as he looked down at his arm. The liquid – flammable acid – ate through the overalls and burned his flesh down to the bones. He screamed louder, his mind unwilling to acknowledge his injury.

Then the flesh grew back. The pain stopped as muscle and sinew stitched together. He held up his arm, checking for any sign of injury. His arm was perfect.

David slapped him on the back. "Welcome to the superpower club. But in case you forgot, there's a flippin' dragon attacking us."

Travis nodded and looked to the horizon. "Christ. I think we've got bigger issues. Look."

Hundreds of people walked towards them. The closer they got, the more Travis realized they were not really people at all. Short reptilian monsters howled at the sky. Larger creatures, purple ogres, walked slowly behind them. Looking up, he saw several other dragons flying low in the air.

Jessica kicked Travis in the shin. "Wake up, pretty boy. We need to not be here."

Travis took one last look at the army, then nodded. The five who had activated the Verdenstab ran as quickly as they could away from the approaching army.

Chapter Thirty-Six

In New York, Josh stared out the window in Wisdom's office at the devastation caused by the Activation. They had been back in New York for almost an hour. The city below was still in chaos. Though the blizzard had ended, a thick blanket of snow covered Central Park. In the distance, several buildings burned, filling the sky with oily smoke. Below, a small plane had crashed into the street. There was no sign of police or any other emergency vehicle.

Garnet stood beside him. Her eyes flowed with tears she did not bother to wipe away. Her lower lip trembled but she kept her eyes focused on the city. It seemed to Josh she was forcing herself to take in every bit of the disaster.

Josh turned at the sound of the door opening behind him. Todd entered, pushing Ms. Ryerson in a wheelchair.

Josh pointed at the chair. "Where did you find that?"

Todd smirked. "There's a hospital two blocks over."

"You went outside in this?" Garnet asked.

Todd shrugged. "I survived a trip to hell. New York isn't that scary anymore. The hard part was trudging this thing through a foot of snow and carrying it up the 50 flights of stairs. People out there are too busy dealing with stuff to notice me. I saw so many car crashes. The hospital was a madhouse. So many people screaming in pain and fear. Doctors and nurses trying to work in the dark."

"We have to help them," Garnet said. "Somehow. We have to help them."

"We will." Josh put his arm around Garnet.

Todd parked the wheelchair beside Wisdom's desk and walked to the window. "This is bad. You guys aren't

American. I don't want to be rude but I don't think you can appreciate what September 11 did to us. It left a wound that won't heal. And now this? I'm worried about my parents. As far as I know, they're still in Anchorage. Maybe they're okay. Maybe this thing didn't reach there. But what I'm really worried about is what happens here tomorrow. How will everyone react when the lights don't come back on?"

Josh frowned. "How do you know they won't?"

"Dude. Do you seriously never watch movies? War of the Worlds? The Matrix? Cars stop in the street. Planes fell from the sky. All our electronics are scrap. That means an EMP. Electromagnetic Pulse. Who knows? The lights may never come back on."

"Let's not panic," Ms. Ryerson said. "For all we know, this only temporary."

Todd inhaled as if about to argue. Then he exhaled slowly. "You're right. I know you're right. It's just…I love New York. It's the greatest city on the planet. They don't deserve to go through this. Not again."

Exhausted, Josh sat down in the chair behind Wisdom's desk. "No one deserves this. I just wish I knew what was happening. I think I really took the Internet for granted."

"The internet may be fine," Ms. Ryerson said. "At least part of it. The American military took precautions to ensure a level of communication after a nuclear event. Wisdom has connections within the military. If we reach out to them we may be able to find the Activation's level of impact."

Garnet nodded. "I hope so. Right now, we have no way of knowing how widespread the damage is. Hell, we don't even know what the device *did*. I've tried reaching out to Jessica telepathically but there's some sort of interference."

Todd frowned. "Do you think she's still…?"

Garnet shook her head. "I don't know. I'm not as strong a telepath as she is. Maybe she's just too far away. That's the worst part. Maybe the others are fine, maybe they're not. There's just no way for us to know."

Ms. Ryerson cleared her throat. "As I said, Wisdom had contacts. This fight isn't over yet, but we can't do anything right now. My legs are broken. I need time to heal. You've all been through hell – literally. I suggest we head to our rooms. Try to get some rest. I'll reach out to Wisdom's contacts in a few hours. We'll find out what's happening."

Todd sat down on Wisdom's desk, staring out at the city. "There's no way I can rest through this. Any idea what time it is?"

Josh looked down at his watch. "My watch still works. I guess whatever happened here didn't affect us because we were still in the Axeinus when it happened. But the time doesn't seem right. According to my watch it's only 3:00 pm."

"How's that possible?" Garnet asked. "It felt like we were in the Axeinus forever."

"Wisdom said time may move differently there." Todd went to the window, his face close the glass. "It's so dark. It's like something has blotted out the sun. Jesus, this is Armageddon. I can almost believe the world ended."

Josh went to the window and put a supportive hand on Todd's shoulder. "The world didn't end. It's changed in ways we don't understand yet, but we're alive. That's something. Come on, Todd. I have something to show you. Garnet, can you give us a light?"

Garnet picked up a pile of papers in the trash and set them on fire.

Using the dim light to guide him, Josh went to the bookshelf at the back of the office. He had to search for a bit before he found the switch. When he pressed it, there was a soft click. Thankfully, the device was mechanical, not electric. Well-oiled gears turned and the wall swung open to reveal Wisdom's secret chamber.

"You've got to be kidding." Todd pushed past Josh into the room. "How long has this been here?"

"Probably since the building was constructed." Garnet stepped into the room, holding her light high. She studied the pictures on the wall. "Some of these look really old. Holy crap! Is that Wisdom standing next to Einstein?"

Josh stood beside her, leaning in to see the picture. "Wow. I'm not sure what's more unbelievable. The fact that he's standing next to Einstein or the fact they're both in bathing suits and laughing hysterically. Can you ever remember Wisdom laughing hysterically?"

"There is much about Wisdom you children don't know." Ms. Ryerson wheeled herself past them to the center table. "I've known Wisdom for the better part of 40 years and there is still much about him I don't know."

"There's no way you've known him for 40 years," Todd said. "Did you meet him when you were four?"

Ms. Ryerson rolled her eyes. "Wisdom is not the only one who is not exactly what he seems. While I'm not immortal, my people have very long lives."

Josh crossed his arms. "What do you mean, 'your people'? You're not human?"

"Who amongst us is?" Ms. Ryerson wheeled past them and went further into the room. "What I am is a story for another day. Garnet, bring your light over here. I think I see something."

Garnet followed. The light faltered as the flames consumed the paper. Still, she managed to illuminate something that twinkled in the torchlight. A metal knob. Ms. Ryerson reached out and touched the handle. A cabinet flipped open, revealing a concealed bookshelf. Josh saw hundreds of books, all leather bound and embossed with gold dates. He pulled one at random off the shelf and flipped through the pages.

"Listen to this," he said. "'Saw Echo today. She was in Pamplona for the running of the bulls. She refused to talk to me but, for a moment, there was a smile on her lips.' These must be Wisdom's journals. This must be what he wanted us to find."

Todd pulled another book off the shelf. He read silently for a moment. Then closed the book.

"What?" Garnet said.

Todd shook his head. "What I read couldn't have been real. There's just no way."

Josh put his own book back on the shelf. "I think I'm beyond being surprised at anything. Today we learned that humans are biomechanical robots invented by Atlanteans, Bigfoot is real, and the Edimmu are not all blood-sucking monsters. Nothing will surprise me."

"Wanna bet?" Todd flipped open the book again and passed it to Josh. "Read that section and try saying that to me again."

Josh looked at the section Todd pointed to. His mouth dropped open. "That can't be real."

"Exactly!" Todd took the book back and put on the shelf. "Can we get out of here? This place is creeping me out."

"What did it say?" Garnet reached for the book but found she couldn't hold it and keep the torch up at the same time. "Come on, tell me what it said."

Josh ran his fingers through his hair. "It said Wisdom had a meeting with a group of aliens called the Nizarians and helped them recover a UFO from the U.S. government in exchange for a promise to stop abducting humans to create hybrids."

Garnet looked at the book in her hand. "I…I don't think I even want to know. We have too much to handle with the Activation right now. I can't even be bothered to think about aliens right now." She moved to put the book back on the shelf. Then she stopped. "You don't suppose that's why he wants us to stay off the moon, do you?"

Josh shrugged. "I don't know. And I'm with you. I don't care. Not right now. We need to find out what the Activation did before we focus on anything else. Ahriman and his army have left the Axeinus. As far as we know, they could have taken over all of Turkey by now. We also need to find out if our friends are still alive. Jessica, David, Elaine. If they're alive, we need to get them back here. Consolidate our resources. And my poor cousin. Travis has no idea what he's involved with. We need to bring him up to speed, find out what he knows."

Garnet looked at the floor. "And there's the issue with your father."

Josh felt the rest of his strength dissipate. "Yeah. We've got him in restraints right now. That's only holding him because he's unconscious."

Garnet sighed. "I've switched off a part of his brain. A normal man would be comatose indefinitely. Your father is far from normal."

"But he's not normal." Josh rubbed his forehead. His head pulsed with the beginning of a headache. "He has powers. He's been through at least the first stages of Eyeness. If he wakes up before we can get him to Candleworks…I don't know if I can actually kill him."

"You won't have to," Garnet said. "I'll know if he wakes up."

Todd cracked his knuckles. "Unless one of his powers is the ability to hide from telepathic scans. Maybe we should have left him in the Axeinus."

Josh shook his head. "He's our only connection to the Orpheans. He was involved in the planning of this thing. We need to know what he knows. I'm tired. So tired. I'm not sure if we screwed up today or if we never had a chance at winning. Maybe you were right, Ms. Ryerson. Maybe we should take a break."

One by one they left Wisdom's secret room. Josh pressed the button to close the door again.

"Get some sleep, children." Ms. Ryerson's wheelchair moved, although she no longer seemed to be pushing it. "We'll find out what happened to the rest of the world soon enough. We've all been through a lot today. We need some time to deal with the fact that Wisdom is gone."

Josh took one last look out the windows at the city on fire. "Everything looks so broken. I'm not sure I'm strong enough for what comes next."

Garnet doused the fire in her hands. "I don't think you have a choice. None of us do. We have to find a way to be strong enough."

Josh smiled and, reaching out, grasped Garnet's hand tightly. 'At least I have you,' he thought. In the short time he had known her, Garnet had come to be the center of his universe, the steady support beam that kept him from falling apart. 'If it wasn't for you I'd just give up. Run away. The world may burn but I still have you.'

Garnet smiled and turned away. Josh realized she was doing him the courtesy of pretending she had not read his thoughts. It made him love her all the more.

Chapter Thirty-Seven

In the fieldbender guild of Karaj Robat, Defksquar sat with the seven leaders of the guild at a round, white marble table. Gilded columns surrounded the otherwise empty room.

"Is it done?"

Defksquar looked over at the man who had spoken. Latimer, the head of the guild, had long white hair and sky blue robes.

"Yes," Defksquar said. "The boy activated the Verdenstab."

"May the Gray One forgive us," Latimer said. "Do you have any idea how many people you just killed?"

Defksquar flinched. "Not as many as would have been killed here if the Quadumvirate got their hands on the Verdenstab. It's beyond their reach now. Our world is safe."

"I would say we're far from safe." A middle-aged man in green-trimmed silver robes pounded the table. "The Sword of Kassandra and the weakening of the Void mean we're closer to war than ever before."

"Easy, Eschandel," Latimer said. "No one here has forgotten about the Sword of Kassandra. But I think we can all admit the presence of the Verdenstab on Maghe Sihre would have made that situation worse. Perhaps we can see this as a victory."

"I don't count the slaughter of millions as a victory," Eschandel said. "Even if those people are from another world. Perhaps the Sage was right when he walked out of here last month."

Defksquar leaned forward and lowered his voice. "If you think that, maybe you should run off and side with him. It's time to decide where your loyalties lie."

Eschandel looked to Latimer, sighed, and then stood. "I think, on this matter, you are right, Defksquar." He walked towards the door.

Latimer stood up as well. "Where do you think you're going?"

Eschandel answered over his shoulder. "Where I should have gone weeks ago. The Sage was right to distrust you, Defksquar. I just wish I'd seen it sooner."

'Damn it,' Defksquar thought as the door closed behind Eschandel. 'How does that idiot inspire so much loyalty? Don't these people see how naïve he is?' Holding his head in his hands, he focused on keeping his breath calm.

Latimer sat down, folding his hands in his lap. "Well, that was disappointing. Eschandel had so much promise. We have an empty seat on the Council now. I know it is unorthodox but I'm wondering if you would join us, Defksquar."

"Excuse me?"

"I know, I know. You're not a fieldbender and you have many duties to attend to, but this plan of yours is ambitious. It could change everything."

Defksquar sighed. "We need new allies, now more than ever. Activating the device was the only way I could think of to get the attention of the Beherskers. Hopefully, wherever they are, they felt the Verdenstab being activated. If so, there's a chance they will come to investigate."

Latimer glanced around the table. All the other fieldbenders nodded in agreement. "And if they are displeased?"

Defksquar folded his arms. "Then the Beherskers can take out their wrath on the humans. The survivors will be far from helpless. There's one fact I was able to hide from the Council and the Orpheans. Anyone with Atlantean DNA, like Wisdom, has the potential for advanced psychic abilities. Those genes were repressed in humans to create a better slave race. In Anomalies, the gene was no longer dormant. That was the source of their power. The Activation turned those genes back on in anyone that survived. It's small consolation for the harm that's been done, but perhaps it will give the humans a fighting chance."

Maybe ash in to reveal more about his life before maghe sihre"

"Very risky," Latimer said. "But smart. Eschandel was right about one thing. The Verdenstab is no longer our immediate concern. There are other forces at work here. It has never been more important for us to be strong."

Defksquar sat quietly for a moment. "I've spent the last 20 years of my life planning on this moment. My work on Earth is done. To be honest, I never really thought about what would happen after this. I'll join on one condition."

"I'm listening," Latimer said.

Defksquar cleared his throat. "There was a slight complication. Amir Durgen and a small army crossed over to Earth. We have no way of knowing how their presence affected the process. If Durgen survived exposure, he will be more powerful than ever. Durgen was a threat before. Now, he would be more than I could handle alone. Thankfully, the Activation disrupted the foramen in Windsor. Until it heals, it can only be opened from this side. But there are other roads between here and Earth. It's only a matter of time before Durgen or someone else comes looking for me. I need you to find a way to hide me from them. Change my energy field so that no one can track me. Permanently. Can you do that?"

Latimer glanced around the table. The other fieldbenders spoke amongst themselves in low, hushed tones. A moment later they nodded and turned back to look at Defksquar.

"What you ask is very…challenging," Latimer said. "A temporary change to a bio-field is easy. I don't know of any way to make such a change permanent but we will find a way. Such a feat could actually work to our benefit. If successful, you'll be able to go places we never could."

Defksquar smiled. "Exactly. If I can't be tracked, I can head into the heart of the Quadumvirate's territory. For the last 20 years I've spied on an alien planet. Maybe it's time I focus on my own world. Thank you, Latimer. You've given me a new mission. I'm in your debt."

Latimer brushed the statement away. "Nonsense. We are in your debt. Despite what Eschandel said, your actions saved millions of lives here. You're a hero."

Defksquar stared at his hands. "I'm fairly certain the people of Earth would disagree with you."

Epilogue

Wisdom stood at the entrance to a cave that looked down on a wooded valley. Tall trees lined either side of a rapidly running river. Birds he did not recognize flew above the treetops. He inhaled deeply. The air felt different in his lungs. He looked up. Two moons hung in the night sky.

"Well, it worked," he said. "I'm definitely not in Kansas." He looked behind him. Uneven green crystal covered the back wall of the cave. Wisdom touched it. "Feels like emerald. I've never seen so much. There must be several tons here. It would be worth a fortune. Of course, that's assuming emerald is as rare here as it is on Earth."

He sat down and leaned his back against the crystal. 'I know absolutely nothing about this world. I've so much to learn.' Wisdom smiled and his eyes grew dim. 'This is a new start for me. A chance to put the past behind me. All the drama and tragedy. Echo is gone. My father's dead. The Anomalies are on their own. I can start again. This time I'll do things properly, not fueled by rage or ignorance. On this world I can be a better man.'

Outside, the crack of lightning drew his attention. Standing, he went to the front of the cave and looked out again at the sky. Dark clouds blew in, blotting out the stars and moons. He watched as rain began to fall. He held his hand out to touch the raindrops. Then he felt something, a presence that was somehow familiar. His heart fluttered for a moment as his eyes searched the area. He noticed a figure below. A man scrambled up the rocks looking for shelter. He headed directly towards Wisdom.

'No time like the present to meet one of the natives. Damn. I don't even know their language. I'll have to communicate telepathically and hope that works.'

As the figure came closer, Wisdom realized he did know the figure.

Defksquar.

He looked around at the shadows. 'What are the odds that I happen to land on the planet in the exact location he'd be in? Either I'm being manipulated or my luck has become amazingly better.' He clenched his fists, covering them in flame. 'But I don't believe in luck.'

He waited until Defksquar was only a few feet below him. Then he threw the fire in his hands. Caught unaware, Defksquar's tunic caught fire. He fell backwards, off the rocks, crashing into a landing midway down the mountain. Wisdom jumped out of the cave and landed, lightly, a few feet from Defksquar. His hands still burned with fire.

"You have much to answer for," Wisdom said.

Defksquar, still prone on the ground, erected a dome of light over his whole body. "You! What are you doing here? How did you get here? There isn't a foramen around for…"

"How I got here isn't important." Wisdom threw a spear of fire at Defksquar. The flame dispersed over the dome, leaving his target unaffected. "Because of you, millions of people are dead. The first thing I will do on this world is avenge them."

Defksquar rose to his feet. The dome moved with him. "On your world. Not mine. What I did saved millions of lives here. I will not apologize for that."

Wisdom smiled. "Good." He opened a teleportation disk beneath Defksquar. The dome did not protect against gravity. Defksquar fell away from the dome's protection and appeared a few feet above Wisdom. He fell, his body crashing into the rocky ledge. Wisdom kicked him in the head, then grabbed him by the throat, lifting him off the ground. "Don't apologize. It's too late for that."

"You're right. It's too late for everything. What's done is done and you can't change it. You can't change the past."

"That, I know all too well." Wisdom set his hands on fire. The flesh around Defksquar's throat burned. Then something unexpected happened. The flesh healed, almost as quickly as it burned. Momentarily distracted, he didn't respond fast enough when Defksquar punched him. His fist struck Wisdom in the chest, pushing him backwards. Defksquar landed on his feet.

"We can't stay here," Defksquar said. "There's a squadron of Umbral Knights chasing me. If we want to survive, we have to work together."

Wisdom slapped Defksquar across the face. "I would rather die than work with you. If something is chasing you, they can have what's left of you when I'm finished."

Defksquar looked down the side of the mountain. "You don't understand. Look for yourself."

Wisdom swallowed his rage for a moment and looked where Defksquar pointed. Fifteen figures in dark armor walked slowly up the mountain. Their eyes glowed blue, the energy leaking out and illuminating the night.

"What are those?" Wisdom asked.

"Umbral Knights. Undead cybernetic soldiers animated with energy from the Void. Once they have your scent, nothing can keep them from finding you. Our only hope is to get to a foramen and jump to another part of the planet."

"There's no 'us' here. I'm certainly not helping you after what you've done." He raised his hands, creating a giant flare of flames. The soldiers looked towards them. They started moving more quickly.

"Idiot!" Defksquar rubbed the back of his head and looked around frantically. "Do you think they'll let you leave? They'll catch your scent, too."

"I can handle myself. How many are there? Fifteen?"

"Those are just the scouts. Look up. There, to the left of that cloud."

Wisdom rolled his eyes and looked where Defksquar pointed. His mouth dropped. "Are those dragons? You have dragons here?"

"They are called wypera. And there are several hundred of them in the area. You can't take them all on."

Wisdom shrugged. "I could try."

Defksquar lunged forward, grabbing Wisdom by the collar. "We have to get out here. I know you hate me. Get past it. Just until we're somewhere safe. I need you and you need me. Like I said, you can't change the past. Time to think about the future."

Wisdom slowly pushed Defksquar back and straightened his shirt. "Someone recently told me that good and evil are subjective. That the hero in one story is the villain in another. Maybe he was right. Maybe you are a hero on this world. Maybe the forces of evil are after you. Or maybe that's the authorities coming to put you in jail. I simply don't know. There's so much I don't know about this world. And there's only one way I can think of learning."

"What are you talking about?"

"I can't go back to my homeworld. You've seen to that. But you're wrong. You can change the past. Not the big stuff, of course, but you can tweak the small details. Maybe if I head back far enough I can still help Earth somehow."

Defksquar's face went pale. "You can't."

"Oh, but I can."

Wisdom opened up a portal and traveled back through time.

***

When Wisdom left, Defksquar's figure flickered. A moment later the illusion dissipated, revealing the real form of the person Wisdom had talked to: a pale-skinned man with snow-white hair. He wore black robes with a sheath attached to his waist; there was no sword in sight.

He turned to a pocket of shadow nearby. "You can come out now. He's gone."

"Do you think it worked?" A woman in a blue dress stepped out of the darkness. Her brown hair was held back in a ponytail.

"Of course it worked. Wisdom did exactly what we needed him to do."

"I hate this plan. I hate everything about it."

"Just remember why we're doing this." The man leaned over the side of the mountain and waved his hand. The illusion of the Umbral Knights faded away. "He felt you for a moment. Did you feel how his heart raced? You have to be more careful. If he learns you're alive…"

"I know."

"I went through a lot of trouble bringing you back. There's a price to pay."

The woman crossed her arms and stared at the ground. "You don't have to remind me. I'm well aware of the price. So what do we do know?"

The man reached up into the sky. With a wave of his hand, the storm disappeared. "We have a little time traveling to do ourselves. Wisdom is a free man on this world. We can't have him making the wrong choices. We'll need to find out how far back he went and help him stay on the path."

"Do we know where the real Defksquar is?"

The man nodded. "Right now he's in Karaj Robat, but he'll be leaving soon. He's on his way to Castle Dispayre. He plans to spy on the Quadumvirate but it won't go the way he plans. He'll be captured in a few weeks."

"I know what he means to you. Are we going to rescue him?"

"No. Wisdom will."

The woman frowned. "I don't understand."

"Not yet. But you will in time. Come on, Echo. We have much to do."

The two figures stepped back into the shadows and were gone.

What's Next – The Worlds of Maghe Sihre and Earth

Have you ever read a book that changed the way you think about fiction? For me, it was actually two books: *Desperation* by Stephen King and *The Regulators* by his pseudonym, Richard Bachman. The amazing thing about these books is they are versions of the same events told simultaneously in two different worlds. *Desperation* is a literary horror novel; *The Regulators* is more pulp fiction. That gave me an idea.

Two worlds. Similar problems. Shared characters. Different genres.

To find out what happens to Wisdom after he travelled back through time, check out A Fallen Hero Rises (available now).

Here's a sneak peak of Chapter One.

Spoiler Alert: The Sage is the new name Wisdom takes on Maghe Sihre.

Chapter One: A Fallen Hero Rises

In the fieldbender guild of Karaj Robat, the Sage closed his eyes in silent prayer. 'Some things you can't come back from. Let's hope this is not one of them.'

His red leather boots stepped quickly over white marble floors as he headed towards the council chamber. Square columns lined the open-air corridor. A cool breeze from the storm raging outside ruffled his high-collared military cape. It did little to cool his temperament. Acolytes in white robes bowed their heads in respect as he passed. He ignored them all, clenching and unclenching his fists, eyes straight ahead. This was no time to pretend he cared about decorum.

Guards flanked either side of the chamber entrance. They stood at attention, hands resting on the hilts of their swords. Both wore ceremonial armor embroidered with the crest of Karaj Robat: a crow superimposed on a red mountain.

The Sage did not slow down as he approached. One guard held up a hand, blocking his path.

"No entry," the guard said. "Fieldbenders only."

The Sage raised one eyebrow and glanced at the other guard.

"Sorry, sir," the second guard said. "He's new. Baubi, stop being an idjit. Let him pass."

The first guard, Baubi, shook his head. "Sorry, Jaymes. I'm not risking my job based on your recommendation. Why would I let this stranger in? I don't even know his name."

Jaymes, the second guard, coughed and went pale. "He's not a stranger. This is the Sage. He's been a consultant to the fieldbenders since before you were born."

Baubi tightened his grip on the hilt. "Stop making fun of how young I am. Besides, the Sage is a position, not a name."

The Sage cleared his throat. "As amusing as you clowns are, I have places to be. I'm expected inside. No one here knows my true name. Names have power. Everyone calls me the Sage. Now are you going to step aside or do I have to push you?"

Baubi started to draw his sword. Jaymes grabbed his arm to stop him.

The Sage's eyes flashed red with an internal flame.

"Please go in, sir," Jaymes said. He quickly opened the twin doors to the chamber. As the doors shut behind him, the Sage heard the two guards continue to bicker.

The meeting had already begun. The council chamber was a large, round room. Tall, gilded columns encircled the room. Between the columns, hundreds of fieldbenders spoke to each other in hushed tones. Most were initiates dressed in white robes. Many blinked rapidly while others nervously glanced at the shadows.

'They look nervous,' the Sage thought. 'That's a good sign. It means they're taking this seriously.'

He pushed through the crowd to reach the white marble table at the center of the room. Like the chamber, it was round. Seven robed men were already seated around the table. These were the leaders of the guild, the ones who had summoned him to the meeting. Two of the chairs around the table were empty. The Sage sat in one and turned to listen to the debate.

"Eschandel, it's just not possible." The speaker, a middle-aged man in green-trimmed silver robes, looked down his nose at a man with slender features in black robes.

"Stop saying that, Sirion." Eschandel slammed his fist against the table. His ice-blue eyes darted from person to person around the table. "For the third time, it is flamin' possible because it's flamin' happened. Sit there and deny it until the moons fall from the sky. It changes nothing. Last night, fifteen Seers had the same vision. A blaze of light flew through space. It slammed into the dimensional prison. Now there's a crack in the Void."

"I think what Sirion is saying is that, perhaps, the Seers are mistaken." This cool voice came from a white-haired man in sky-blue robes. Though much older than the first two speakers, his eyes were sharp and clear. "We need more than their word before we panic."

Eschandel took a deep breath. "As I was about to say before Sirion stuck his head in the sand…again…we have more proof. I present Bender Mikhel from DunDegore. His report should shut you up."

The white-haired man cleared his throat.

"Sorry, Latimer." Eschandel hung his head and rubbed the back of his neck. "His report should help clarify things."

The white-haired man, Latimer, smiled and nodded to show his support.

The Sage turned as a new figure stepped forward. Like the majority of the crowd, this man wore the white robes of an initiate; however, his robes were dirty, the hem caked with mud. He had obviously been traveling.

"I'm Mikhel," the man said. "I can't speak of the Void directly but my guild has reason to believe it is damaged. It's the only explanation for what we found. Something fell out of the Void."

For a moment, there was silence.

Then the room erupted into curses and shouts of disbelief.

Latimer lifted a hand and everyone hushed.

"Please," Eschandel said, "continue."

Mikhel wiped sweat from the edge of his neck as he looked around the room. "I'm part of the research team from DunDegore. As you know, we've explored the ruins for decades. The old Behersker city goes down for miles. We've only uncovered the first 50 levels. Usually we find trinkets – tools, dishware, data disks. Yesterday we found something else."

"Spit it out already," Sirion said. "We don't need an archeology lesson."

"Yes, sir." Mikhel's ears turned red. He glanced at Latimer but, unable to look the leader of the guild in the eye, he focused on Eschandel. "We found a sword. At first, we assumed it was a sculpture, perhaps part of a statue we had yet to discover. No one's ever found a Behersker weapon. There's considerable doubt they actually had conventional weapons. But it proved to be anything but ornamental. The blade was translucent yet harder than any metal, even darkstone. The hilt was opaque and appeared to be crafted from onyx. It's also impervious to damage. We tested it against fire, electricity, acid and blunt force. No effect. When we tested its reaction to fieldbending we began to realize exactly what we'd found. It seemed to eat every spell we threw it at. The archeologists asked me to examine the sword because of my area of expertise. Starfall."

"By the Oak." Latimer covered his mouth with trembling fingers, eyes no longer clear. He glanced at Eschandel. The younger fieldbender nodded and closed his eyes.

"From the look on your face, sir, I see you understand." This time Mikhel was able to look Latimer in the eyes. "The sword has inscriptions visible only when exposed to Akashic energy. The script wasn't Behersker. It was Sirian. The sword has a name."

"The Sword of Kassandra," Latimer said.

Mikhel nodded.

The room became deadly silent as if everyone had forgotten how to breathe.

Sirion shook his head. "Preposterous. The Sword of Kassandra is locked in the Void."

"Correction," Eschandel said. "It *was* locked away. It's not anymore. If you want more evidence let me introduce you to Leinda Farthing. She's our ambassador to the geognosts. She studied with Defksquar some years ago, which makes her the best expert available. I'll let her explain why she's here."

A woman dressed in deer-hide pantaloons and an unbleached tunic stepped out from the crowd. Her long brown hair was pulled back in a tight ponytail. A tribal tattoo decorated the length of her neck: a dragon.

"The head of my guild sent me here to deliver a warning," she said. "I'm sure you all know we specialize in manipulations of foramen and the magnetic subweb of our planet. We are highly attuned to inter-dimensional activity. Two days ago there was activity like we've never felt before. After hours of investigation we discovered the cause. Something came into our world. Think of it like a meteor that smashed through the walls of our dimension instead of crashing down through our atmosphere. Whatever it was, wherever it came from, it didn't close the portal it created. As long as it remains open, other things may enter our world."

"And what say you, Sage?" Latimer stared down at his hands.

The Sage cleared his throat. "I say Sirion needs female companionship more regularly. There is nothing more annoying than someone who claims to be a skeptic but is truly a fascist. Whatever happened, I felt it too. Two days ago. It was similar to the opening of a foramen but more…raw. Dangerous. I have no idea what caused it and, as you know, I despise not knowing. We all knew there was a possibility the Void wouldn't hold forever. If there is any chance it's compromised we have to alert the

Great Castles. You should send envoys to the Valgt'til and the Redgraves."

"I tend to agree." Latimer placed his hands, palm down, on the table. "At worst, we appear over-prepared for battle. But if we say nothing and there is a crack in the Void, well, we can't take that risk."

Sirion grumbled. "I'll have you know I get female companionship regularly."

Eschandel chuckled, a wide grin on his face.

"Hardly the most pressing issue at hand," Latimer said. "Sirion, I'll send you back to DunDegore with our friend Mikhel. Help verify it's truly the Sword of Kassandra. Your skepticism will come in handy. If it is, we need to safeguard it. Something that powerful in the wrong hands could be disastrous."

"You mean the Quadumvirate, I suppose."

Latimer stood and looked around the crowd. "We need to move quickly but keep this quiet. By any oath you hold sacred, this news cannot leave this room. Trust no one. The Quadumvirate has spies everywhere. I'll head to Castle Grygar myself. Eschandel, I'll leave you in charge in my absence." He turned to a middle-aged man in red robes, "Bahrza, I'll send you to Castle Redgrave. Your connections in the court will get us a quick audience with the royal family."

The Sage raised his hand before speaking. "It would probably be in our best interest to notify the Nizarians as well."

Latimer nodded. "That's assuming they're not behind this. Gods only know what that race is capable of. I have someone I trust who will deliver the message. From this moment on, be on alert. The Sword of Kassandra may be the least of our worries. There are far worse things imprisoned in the Void. If it's cracked, Dispayre could break free."

The Sage bit his inner cheek. "And that means war."

Joseph Murphy was born and raised in Ontario, Canada. He earned his geekdom at an early age. He read X-Men comics from at the age of 8 and it only went downhill from there.

As a teenager he wrote short stories and wanted to be the next Stephen King. Instead of horror, however, he kept writing fantasy stories. After surviving high school as a goth with a purple mohawk, he studied English and Creative Writing at the University of Windsor.

When not writing, Joseph works as Lead Accounting instructor at Everest College. He also lectures to other businesses on outside-the-box marketing. He lives in Windsor, ON (right across the stream from Detroit, Michigan) with his husband, two cats, and shy-but-friendly ghost.